A King Production presents…

The Legacy Part II

Keep The Family Close...

A Novel

JOY DEJA KING

Cover concept by Joy Deja King
Cover Model: Joy Deja King

Library of Congress Cataloging-in-Publication Data;
King, Deja Joy
The Legacy Part 2: a novel/by Joy Deja King

For complete Library of Congress Copyright info visit;
www.joydejaking.com Twitter: @joydejaking

A King Production
P.O. Box 912, Collierville, TN 38027

A King Production and the above portrayal logo are trademarks of A King Production LLC

This Book is Dedicated To My:

Family, Readers, and Supporters.
I LOVE you guys so much. Please believe that!!

The Legacy...

A Trilogy

"The Cruelest Thing About Betrayal,
Is It Never Comes From Your Enemies.
It Comes From The Ones You Love..."

~Unknown~

A KING PRODUCTION

The Legacy Part II

Keep The Family Close...

A Novel

Joy Deja King

Chapter One

Edge Of Darkness

Ashton's eyelids felt heavy, as she struggled to see her surroundings. Everything appeared blurry and out of focus. "Where am I?" she mumbled, trying to lift her body up from the bed. "What in the..." her words slurred and she moaned out in pain. The quick movement she made, caused her right arm to jerk back, due to the restraint clasping her wrist. She reached over with her left hand and desperately tried to free herself but it would take a key to unlock the metal handcuff, that had her chained to the bed pole.

"You need to relax. No sense working yourself into a frenzy." A man with a thick Spanish accent, entered the room and said.

"Who are you and why do you have me chained to a bed?" Ashton lifted her head, carefully moving her upper body forward, making sure not to cause additional pain to right arm. "And can you turn on the light, so I can see your face?" she muttered, still feeling drained from the aftereffects of the drug given to her during the abduction.

"Enough questions. I'll be back later on to bring you some food."

"Food? I don't want you to feed me! I want to go home!" Ashton tried to yell but her voice was raspy and dry from a lack of water.

"Have it your way but I suggest you eat. Get comfortable, you'll be here for a while."

Ashton wanted to shout for the man to stop but she was too weak. When the door slammed, she laid her head back down on the pillow. Ashton began to doze back off, fighting to remember how she got here.

Clayton had taken his time getting to Brennan's, for the bogus business meeting he'd set up. He wanted to make sure he left enough time, for their father to catch his mistress with his own son. Clayton imagined how incensed the family patriarch would be, to realize he and Kasir were bedding the same woman. He laughed thinking about it, as he pulled up to the restaurant. But instead of witnessing an all-out brawl he predicted between his father and brother, the parking lot was roped off. Police officers had flooded the scene to prevent unauthorized people from entering the area and potentially contaminating it. There were shell casings spread across the pavement.

"Excuse me, I need to go inside the restaurant," Clayton said, to the officer who was standing at what had become an only one entrance/exit.

"This is a restricted area. No one is allowed in or out of the restaurant at this time. We're currently processing a crime scene."

"I understand that," Clayton said, noticing one of the crime scene investigators kneeling beside a puddle of blood. "But my father and brother are in there waiting for me."

"Then I suggest you give them a call and let them know, you won't be able to make it. Now excuse me, I'm working," the officer said smugly.

Clayton knew it would be futile to argue with the cop, so he headed back to his car. "Damn!" He shook his head in frustration. "I bet my entire plan was a bust! All cause some trigger happy dumb fucks decided to have a shootout in a parking lot!" Clayton fumed, slamming his car door. As he was about to pull off, he noticed his father was calling him. "Dad, I was about to call you.

Some crazy..."

"You need to come to Houston Methodist Hospital...now!" Allen yelled, cutting Clayton off.

"What's going on...did something happen to mother?" Clayton's heart began pounding.

"No. Your mother is fine. It's Kasir. He's been shot." Clayton's mouth dropped, turning to look at the crime scene he just left. Realizing the puddle of blood he was staring at, belonged to his own brother. "I'm on the way."

As Allen was finishing his call with Clayton, he noticed Crystal speaking to one of the nurses. He knew it wouldn't be wise to cause a public spectacle, so Allen waited for the nurse to leave before walking over.

"What the hell are you doing here and why were you at Brennan's with my son?"

Although Allen spoke in a low and extremely calm tone, there was no denying the fury in his eyes. Crystal had never seen her former lover look at her with such malice. She felt a lump in her throat, which caused her to hesitate answering his question.

"I wanted to see how Kasir is doing." Crystal's voice cracked due to fear.

"It's none of your concern. He's in there fighting for his life because of you."

"That's not true!" she cried.

"My son took a bullet trying to shield you. How long have you been seeing Kasir?" Crystal swallowed hard, not wanting to respond to Allen's question. "Answer me!" he gripped her wrist tightly.

"For a few months now?" Crystal admitted.

"Does he know about us?" the grimacing stare Allen gave her, sent a chill down Crystal's back.

"No. He has no idea. I planned on telling him though."

"You will do no such thing. You will turn around and leave this hospital and never see my son again."

"Please don't do this. Can I at least wait until after he gets out of surgery? Pleaaaase!" Crystal pleaded.

"You need to leave now. My wife could show up here any minute. She cannot see you here. Now leave, before this turns ugly," Allen warned.

Crystal ran off in tears. She wanted to stay and be there for Kasir when he got out of surgery but she had no intentions of going to war with Allen Collins. Her encounter with him, had left her traumatized. Crystal didn't even recognize the man who was killing her softly, with just the way he glared at her.

"What are you doing here?!" the sound of Clayton's voice, shook Crystal completely out of her thoughts.

"I just got grilled by your father. I'm not about to go through it again with you!" she snapped.

"Yes the hell you are!" They were near the entrance of the hospital, so Clayton grabbed Crystal by her arm and pulled her outside.

"Get your hands off of me!" she yelled, tired of being manhandled by the Collins' men.

"You better keep your voice down and answer my questions."

"Or what...you're gonna threaten me like your father did?" she spit.

"My dad threatened you?"

"Yes. He told me to leave the hospital before his wife showed up and..." Crystal's eyes watered up.

"And what?" Clayton pressed.

"I better stay away from Kasir. He even blamed me for Kasir getting shot," she continued as the tears trickled down her cheeks.

"I know you're upset but try to calm down and tell me exactly what happened," Clayton said, softening his approach. He could see Crystal was upset and strong arming her wasn't the way to proceed. "Do you need to sit down?"

"No," she said shaking her head before continuing. "Kasir and I were leaving Brennan's and then your father showed up. Out of nowhere, some dark colored van pulls up and starts shooting. Your father's driver Jackson, pulled up quickly and started shooting at the van. It was all happening so fast," her bottom lip trembled. "I guess I wasn't moving fast enough because right before one of the stray bullets hit me, Kasir jumped in front. Next thing I know, Kaisr is laying on the ground in a pool of blood."

"Fuck!" Clayton roared. "How bad is it?"

"It's bad." Crystal broke down and wailed.

"I have to go be with my brother." Clayton said, turning to go back inside the hospital.

"Wait!" Crystal called out.

"What is it?"

"Please call me the moment Kasir is out of surgery and let me know how he's doing."

"Okay."

"Don't okay me, Clayton. Promise me...promise me!" she demanded.

"I promise. Now go. We've been talking long enough," Clayton said, not wanting anyone to see them together.

"I'll go but you better keep your promise, or I will be back. I don't care what you or your father say," Crystal stated before storming off.

Clayton wasn't worried about Crystal's indirect threat, Kasir was his only concern. Even the slightest possibility of losing him, had Clayton in his feelings. He was the only brother he had and Clayton knew there would be hell to pay if Kasir didn't survive.

Chapter Two

From Fantasy Back To Reality

Karmen felt a pair of soft lips kissing her shoulder. His touch had become all too familiar in only a matter of hours.

"You were sleeping so peacefully. I almost hated to wake you," Caesar said, as he continued to sprinkle his kisses up Karmen's slender neck.

"Oh really," she giggled, sitting up in the bed. "And

here I thought we both had fallen asleep. You've been awake all this time?" Karmen asked.

"Nah, you mos def put me to sleep. The only reason I woke up, was because your phone been going off nonstop."

"Well now that you woke me up, why don't you put me back to sleep," she teased.

"Babe, I was just waiting for you to say the word," Caesar smiled. "Do you wanna check your phone first? Someone is trying hard to get in touch with you."

"They can wait. I'm right where I want to be." Karmen leaned in, gliding the tip of her nail across Caesar's chiseled chest.

"How did I get this lucky," Caesar uttered, brushing his lips against Karmen's, which led to their tongues intertwined in a passionate kiss.

Caesar slid his dick back inside of Karmen with ease, as her pussy was still wet. Her inner walls felt like silk to him, so he wanted to take his time with each stroke, savoring the warmth.

"Damn, you feel so fuckin' good," Caesar moaned, dying to cum inside of her at that very moment but he didn't want the feeling of euphoria to end. Instead of giving into his urge, he laid down on his back and let Karmen ride. He stared in awe while she straddled him, admiring her feminine, soft curves that was also perfectly toned, due to her years of dancing. Caesar had imagined the sex being great but not this immaculate. Their bodies were on one accord, creating the perfect harmony. Caesar and Karmen were making love, as if they were soulmates instead of new lovers.

"Have you been able to get in touch with your mother?" Allen barked at Clayton, when he came back into the waiting room.

"Not yet. I've been texting and calling but no response. I'm not sure what's going on with her. You don't think, whoever shot at you and Kasir has gone after mom?" he asked.

"Damn! I pray not." Allen shook his head. Clayton observed dread immediately spread over his father's face, as if this was the first time that possibility even crossed his mind. "Keep trying to reach your mother. I'm going to find the doctor. See if there's any updates on Kasir."

"What about Ashton? I can't reach her either," Clayton said.

"Keep calling!" Allen shouted, as he left the room.

After leaving another message for his mother and not being able to get in touch with his sister, Clayton decided to call Damacio.

"Hello."

"Damacio, this is Clayton."

"Surprised to get a call from you, since our families no longer do business together."

"Trust me, I have no interest in hearing your voice," Clayton scoffed, brushing some sort of dust particle off his suit jacket. "I'm trying to locate Ashton. There's a family emergency and I need to speak with her. She's not answering her phone. Do you know where she is?"

"No, I haven't been able to get in touch with her either," Damacio admitted.

"You haven't been in touch with your wife? What sort of marriage you got," Clayton mocked.

"Save your fuckin' sarcasm. I don't keep a leash on Ashton. She's my wife not a pet. She's free to have a life."

"Whatever. If you get in touch with her before I do, please tell her to call me. It's urgent," he stressed.

"It sounds serious...what happened?" Damacio questioned.

"Nothing I care to share with you. Just tell my sister to call me," Clayton said, before hanging up.

Clayton began pacing the floor. Initially it was only a passing thought, that something had happened to his mother. But now, not being unable to get in touch with his sister too, had him on edge. He was prepared to call the police but then his mother showed up.

"Mom!" Clayton walked over and gave her a hug. "You have no idea, how relieved I am to see you."

"I came the moment I got your message," Karmen said, hugging her son tightly. "How's Kasir?" she asked panic stricken.

"Dad went to find the doctor. Kasir might still be in surgery, I'm not sure. I'd be lying if I said I wasn't worried."

"How did this even happen?" Karmen cried.

Before Clayton had a chance to answer, Allen came back in the waiting room. "Where were you?" he asked his wife in an accusatory tone. "We've been trying to get in touch with you for hours."

"I'm sorry. I was at one of those all day spa retreats and I didn't have access to my phone," Karmen lied. "I got here as soon as I heard. Have you spoken to the doctor...what did they say?" she questioned, wanting to get off the topic of her whereabouts.

"Yeah dad, what did the doctor say?"

"Kasir's out of surgery but his injuries are still critical. They're keeping him on the ventilator until he's strong enough to breathe on his own," Allen explained.

"Can we see him?" Karmen wanted to know.

"The nurse will be here shortly to let us know when we can go in. Right now, we just need to remain positive," Allen said, taking his wife's hand but she pulled away.

"I'm going to try calling Ashton again. I'll be right back," Clayton told his parents.

"I come home from being out of town and you're not there. I can't get in touch with you for hours and when you finally show up, you don't want me touching you. What is your problem?" Allen questioned after Clayton left out.

"This isn't the time."

"What do you mean, this isn't the time? If there's something bothering you, I want to know what it is?" Allen persisted.

"You're my problem." Karmen glared at her husband and stated defiantly.

"Excuse me! What in the world are you talking about?"

"Your lies...I'm sick of them," Karmen spewed.

"I haven't lied to you."

"Look at you. Your arrogance allows you to lie with no shame. Do you even have a conscious anymore? Don't bother answering."

"Karmen, where is all this hostility coming from?" Allen reached out and grabbed his wife's arm as she turned away.

"Don't touch me!" Karmen yanked her arm away. "I saw the video of you having sex with your mistress, during your so called business trip," she shouted, right when the nurse walked in.

"Mr. and Mrs. Collins, you can go in to see your son now," the nurse informed them, pretending not to have heard their intense exchange.

"Thank you." Karmen said politely.

"This conversation isn't over!" Allen barked. She ignored her husband and instead followed the nurse out the room. Karmen was done with him and their marriage.

Chapter Three

Never Recover

Alejo had remained in seclusion at his luxury cottage in Little Palm Island for the past several months. Initially, he believed his isolation was only temporary but getting rid of his enemy was taking longer than he anticipated.

"Is he dead?" Alejo questioned, when Gustaf arrived. He had been sitting on his front porch, overlooking the beach, smoking his cigar, eagerly awaiting the news of his former friend and colleague's death.

"Mr. Hernandez, unfortunately my men were unable to kill him. His driver pulled up and intervened."

Alejo let out a deep sigh. "So Allen Collins is still alive. How unfortunate for you, Gustaf."

"But sir, his son was hit." Gustaf hoped that would spare his boss from punishing him. "We're almost positive his injuries were fatal," he added.

Alejo put down his cigar and glanced up at Gustaf. "Which son?"

"I'm not sure but I'm working on getting an inside connect at the hospital he was taken to."

"Ya parale con tus mamadas!"

"Sir, I'm not bullshitting you...I swear. I will make this right," Gustaf swore.

"You better. Don't come back to my home until Allen Collins is dead!" Alejo bellowed, in his thick Spanish accent. "He must pay for not only disrupting my life but for the death of Gilberto, who was my family."

"I understand and I promise to make sure it's done. I'm on my way to Houston now, to oversee everything myself. No more mistakes."

"Good...now go," Alejo waved his hand dismissively. "I no longer want to look at you. Now leave me."

Alejo's hatred for Allen, had been growing like an incurable disease. It was now spreading rapidly throughout his body, showing no signs of slowing down. It seemed the cure would only come, after his enemy was dead and buried

"Staring at the phone ain't gonna make it ring no quicker," Remi cracked, tossing popcorn in her mouth.

"I invited you over to help me feel better, not remind me how fucked up my situation is right now," Crystal complained.

"If you watch this funny ass movie on tv, instead of manning the phone, you would feel better."

"I'm in no mood to laugh," Crystal said, taking a sip of her wine. "I should be at the hospital with Kasir. This ain't right!" she exclaimed, getting up from the couch.

"I know you not going to the hospital?" Remi asked, pressing pause on the remote, before following Crystal into her bedroom.

"Yes I am," she stated stubbornly. Grabbing some jeans from her closet.

"No the hell you ain't!" Remi ripped the jeans out of Crystal's hand. "I get you worried about dude but you need to fall back. You said it was too dangerous for you to be at the hospital."

"Maybe I exaggerated a little. I don't think I'm in danger anymore."

Remi eyed Crystal disbelievingly, staring her up and down. "Do the police have the men responsible for shooting at you and Kasir in custody?"

"No, not yet." There was a hint of uneasiness in Crystal's voice.

"You told me the police advised you to stay away from the hospital because they believed your life could still be in danger. If the shooters aren't in custody, then what has changed?"

"Kasir would want me by his side. I was with him when he got shot. He was protecting me!" Crystal yelled.

"If Kasir was protecting you, then he damn sure wouldn't want you putting your life in jeopardy. You said his brother was gonna get in touch with you. Why can't you wait for his call?" Remi asked.

"Oh please! His snake ass brother isn't gonna call me," Crystal mumbled.

"Girl, what the fuck is really going on with you and where is the anger towards his brother coming from?"

Crystal gritted her teeth. She never planned on coming clean with Remi but she was fed up with all the lies. "I haven't been honest with you," she finally admitted.

"I figured as much. Are you ready to tell me what's really going on?"

"Where do I even start," Crystal huffed, flopping down on her bed. She stared up at the ceiling, hoping after her confession, she would miraculously feel better.

"You can start by telling me if your life is in danger or not. Don't have me over here scared for no damn reason," Remi smacked.

"I'm sorry for worrying you, Remi. I was so upset when I called you and when you were asking me all those questions, I got flustered. I was too ashamed to tell you the truth, so I lied. The police didn't tell me to stay away from the hospital, Kasir's father did."

"Kasir's father...why would he have beef with you? Oh goodness, does he think you're the reason his son got shot? That's fucked up," Remi said sympathetically, sitting down on the bed next to Crystal.

"Remember the married man I was seeing..."

"Hell yeah! He had you staying in that sick ass crib. Some of the best pics on my Instagram page was taken in that high rise penthouse," Remi bragged, until noticing the frown on her friend's face. "Crystal, I didn't mean to make you feel bad. Your new spot is super cute too."

"Oh girl, I ain't thinking about that," Crystal shook her head, tossing the throw pillow across the bed. "The married man I was seeing, is Kasir's father."

"No fuckin' way! You've been having sex with father and son...that's disgusting!" Remi uttered.

"That right there," Crystal cringed, pointing her finger directly at Remi, "Is the reason I didn't want to tell you the truth."

"My bad! I wasn't expecting you to say that. You caught me off guard."

"Well imagine how fuckin' mortified I was, when the truth slapped me in the face."

"So, you had no idea?" Remi gave Crystal a baffled stare.

"Of course not! I only found out earlier today before the shooting. The entire time I was having lunch with Kasir, I debated if I should tell him the truth. But I couldn't do it."

"How did you even find out?"

"Kasir's brother." Crystal's face screwed up.

"Hence the snake ass comment," Remi presumed.

"One reason but trust, there are so many more. We can have that conversation another day."

"Good because I'm still having a hard time processing the father/son dynamic." Remi rolled her eyes. "I get why you're stressing out but you need to stay far away from the hospital."

Crystal buried her face in the pillow, feeling defeated. She wanted to believe Allen wouldn't have the nerve to tell his son the truth about their relationship but she couldn't shake the gaze of disdain her former lover gave her at the hospital. Wondering what he might do next, made her fearful. Crystal adored Kasir and if there was the slightest chance they could be together, she didn't want to risk losing him, at least not under these circumstances. But more than anything, she just wanted to make sure he would be okay, after getting shot multiple times.

"I won't go to the hospital but if I don't hear from Clayton by tomorrow then..."

"Then what?" Remi asked, as Crystal sat on her bed looking like she was lost in space.

"Then you'll go to the hospital and find out how Kasir's doing."

"Oh hell nah! I'm not going nowhere near that hospital."

"Why not? They don't know you. You can go in, ask a few questions and walk right back out. Never raising any suspicion."

"You don't think one of his family members are going to wonder, who is this random chick, asking questions about Kasir?"

"Remi, I've witnessed you talk your way out of some of the craziest bullshit. Schmoozing with a few nurses at the hospital, will be a breeze for you. Please!" Crystal begged.

"If you don't hear from his brother tomorrow, then I'll go but only if his brother doesn't call," Remi agreed.

"Thank you so, so much!" Crystal hugged Remi enthusiastically. "My mind won't rest until I know how Kasir is doing."

"I'll go but only because, if you hightail yo' ass over to that hospital, all hell will break loose and you don't need the drama."

"I agree but I know Kasir would want me by his side."

"I seriously doubt he'll feel that way, when he finds out you been fuckin' his daddy?" Remi mocked. "Personally, I think you should throw the whole family away. Forget both of them and find a new man," she advised.

"I can't do that. Kasir means way too much to me."

"Then be careful. I don't see anything positive coming from your relationship with him. You think it's bad now, if you continue your relationship with Kasir, it's only going to get worse," Remi warned.

"Mom, you should go home and get some rest," Clayton said to his mother, who hadn't left her son's bedside. "You've been here all night. Have you slept at all?"

"I dozed off a few times but I want to be here in case your brother wakes up."

"I understand but I spoke to the nurse before I came in and they have Kasir in a drug induced coma. If they notice the swelling recede, then they'll try to lighten up the coma to see if he can come back and what his level of function is. So you have time to go home and get some rest." Clayton explained to his mother as he held her hand.

"If he doesn't pull through, I don't know what I'll do," Karmen's voice trembled.

"Don't think like that. Kasir is tough. You go home and I'll stay here with him. You need to stay strong for Kasir."

Karmen nodded her head in agreement. She knew Clayton was right. "I'll go home, take a shower and get some rest. I'll be back in a few hours."

"Take your time. If anything comes up, I'll call

you...I promise." Clayton gave his mother a hug and kiss.

"Okay," Karmen said, getting her purse from the chair. "Have you spoken to Ashton? I thought she would've been here by now."

"Not yet but I spoke to Damacio. Ashton went out of town and lost her phone. He did speak with her and she's on her way back home," Clayton lied.

"Good. Kasir needs all of our support. We have to be together as a family," Karmen emphasized.

"And we will be. We also have to remain strong and take care of ourselves, so you go. I'll be here when you get back."

Clayton hated to lie to his mother about Ashton. But with one child in the ICU, he couldn't stomach seeing the pain in her eyes, when he admitted her only daughter and his sister, was missing. Clayton knew he couldn't keep the truth from his mother much longer but he was praying Ashton would miraculously appear before his lie unraveled.

"Damn, let this be the good news I've been waiting for," Clayton mumbled, when he noticed Damacio calling. "Hello."

"I think Ashton's been taken." Damacio's words felt like a sharp knife slicing open Clayton's throat.

"What do you mean taken?" he asked, stepping out of Kasir's room.

"My men located Ashton's car. Her purse, car key and a pair of sunglasses were found next to it in the parking lot where she had a hair appointment." Damacio went silent for a moment. "I have to find my wife, Clayton. We need to put our differences aside and work together on this."

"Not Ashton." Clayton's voice went lifeless. "This will kill my mother. The family would never recover." He seemed to fade away into a daze.

"Then help me find her," Damacio said, trying to keep his cool. "Clayton, did you hear what I said?" Still there was no response. "Clayton!" he shouted through the phone. "Answer me!"

"I'm here," he finally spoke up. "Of course we'll work together. I need to bring my sister home."

"Good. My men are working on some possible leads but I want to discuss a few things with you. Can you come over?"

"I can't. I'm at the hospital with Kasir."

"Did something happen to your brother?"

"Yeah, he was shot yesterday."

"I'm sorry to hear that. I always liked Kasir. How's he doing?"

"Not good but he's alive, so we're staying optimistic."

"Do you think Kasir's shooting has anything to do with Ashton's disappearance?" Damacio asked.

"I don't know what to think right now. In less than twenty-four hours, my entire family seems to be falling apart."

"Clayton, you're dealing with a lot right now. I can

come to you," Damacio suggested.

"No. If my father or mother sees you here, they'll know something is wrong. I don't want my mother to find out about Ashton, unless I have no other choice," Clayton sighed, knowing if that happened, it meant he knew his sister was never coming home again. "Meet me at that restaurant across the street from Houston Methodist in an hour."

"I'll be there. In the meantime, keep this conversation between us," Damacio said, before ending the call.

Clayton went back into his brother's room after finishing his call with Damacio. He had no intentions or desire to tell anyone, what they discussed. The one person he did wish to confide in, was unavailable, Clayton thought standing by his brother's side.

"Damn Kasir, I need you right now. I would give anything for you to wake up and tell me what to do. I'm used to making messes, not cleaning them up. That's your specialty. I don't know what's killing me more. Seeing you lying here, hooked up to a ventilator, or our baby sister missing, not knowing, if she's hurt or even worse...dead."

Clayton took a moment of silence and prayed for his loved ones. They needed to keep the family close, now more than ever.

Chapter Four

Time Isn't On Your Side

"Dinner time," the man known to Ashton as Chi said, bringing her a tray of food. Like clockwork, he would always bring dinner, at exactly 6:15pm. At first, Ashton wouldn't touch the food but by day three, she was starving to the point of becoming delusional.

"How many days have I been here?" Ashton asked, taking a bite of the grill chicken sandwich.

"This is week two," Chi told her, putting down the DVD's Ashton requested.

"What's your end game? You're feeding me good food, getting my favorite movies and you even removed the handcuff. You said this wasn't about a ransom, so then what?" Ashton continued munching on her French fries, waiting for Chi to answer her question.

"Like I told you before, all you need to know is I have no intentions of harming you. Think of it, as me keeping you safe."

"Safe from what? I have a husband and a family, I'm positive is worried sick about me. Why won't you tell me how long you plan on keeping me here...or don't you have any intentions of letting me go?"

"You will know what you need to, when the time is right," Chi said, waiting as Ashton finished up the last of her meal. "I'll see you in the morning." He took the tray and walked out the room, leaving his prisoner with more questions than answers.

Ashton got out of bed and walked over to the window that was completely boarded up. She had no way of knowing if it was day or night because she didn't have access to the outside world. She was left to guess the time of day, based on when her meals were served.

What does this man want from me? Ashton thought to herself, picking up one of the magazines Chi left for her. She flipped through the pages of InStyle, wondering if her days of wearing designer threads were over. *Why me? If this isn't about money then what? Maybe*

Chi's bullshitting and the plan is to kill me. Hell, I don't even know if Chi is this man's real name, she became frustrated, tossing down the magazine.

The not knowing was taking the biggest toll on Ashton's psyche. She couldn't stomach being kept hidden in a room, not sure if she would live or die.

"I don't want you to go," Caesar said, kissing Karmen's neck.

"I have to get back to the hospital and be with my son." Karmen got out of bed and started getting dress as Caesar watched thinking what he could say to make her stay.

"I understand you want to be with your son but maybe you can come back later on tonight?" he asked.

"I'll be at the hospital until late."

"I can wait up. You can always spend the night."

"You know I can't do that," Karmen said, buttoning up her blouse.

"You keep saying that but you never tell me why. You said your marriage is over, so what's the problem? Why can't you stay here with me?" Caesar wanted to know.

Karmen stopped what she was doing and stared at Caesar who was still in the bed. She was ready to go because she hated to be away from Kasir for more than a couple hours during the day. But Karmen genuinely cared about the man, who'd become her escape for the past couple weeks and felt he deserved an explanation.

"My marriage is over but my family is in turmoil right now. Kasir is still in a coma and we haven't been able to get in contact with Ashton. This isn't the time to disrupt our lives even more, by telling my husband, I won't be coming home because I'll be staying at my lover's house."

"I get it."

"Do you really? Most single people, really have no clue how complicated marriage can be."

"You're right and I know me wanting you to be here, when you're dealing with so much, probably seems very selfish but I want you," Caesar stated.

"And I want you too," Karmen admitted, sitting back down on the bed next to Caesar. She stroked the side of his chiseled face. She gazed into his deep, dark eyes. He had the bone structure of a model but his stare was discerning as if he'd seen and lived an arduous life.

"I believe you but I also know, family is your first priority. I don't want you to stay with your husband because you feel obligated to keep your family together. You have the right to move on and be happy with me," he stressed.

"And when the time is right, we will be together. I promise," she said, leaning in and kissing Caesar.

Caesar planned to guarantee Karmen kept her promise. When he first met her, he saw her as this perfect woman who seemed out of his reach. But now, that he got her in his bed and let Karmen in his heart, Caesar had no intentions of letting her go.

"I can't keep this from my parents any longer, especially my mother," Clayton said, pacing the living room floor, at the home Damacio shared with his sister.

"My men are so close to finding out what happened to Ashton. I know this is difficult but all I'm asking is for a couple more days. If my wife isn't home by Friday, then you do what you have to do," Damacio stated.

"A couple days could make all the difference, if my sister lives or dies," Clayton said, loosening his tie. "My father might be able to help. He has a lot of connections."

"Listen, we've been working together for this long without your father. A couple more days is all I'm asking for."

"Okay," Clayton reluctantly agreed. "But if Ashton is dead, my mother and father will never forgive me for keeping her disappearance from them."

"I believe my wife is still alive but if I'm wrong, then put it all on me. I'm the one who's been lying to your parents. They never have to find out you knew the truth," Damacio explained to Clayton.

"But I'll have to live with the truth. We keep a lot of secrets in our family but the one thing we were all on the same page about, was protecting Ashton. If she dies, it means I failed her," Clayton said, with a heavy heart.

"Then I failed her too," Damacio refuted, holding up a picture of the two of them on their wedding day. "She's my wife. I'm supposed to protect Ashton and I didn't. Let me be the one to carry the guilt."

"I have to get back to the hospital," Clayton announced abruptly. "My mother just sent me a text saying there's been a change in Kasir's condition."

Damacio placed the photo he was holding, back down on top of the piano, focusing his attention on Clayton. "I hope everything's okay with Kasir." he said, walking him to the door. "You focus on your brother and let me find Ashton. I love her very much and will do everything within my power to bring her home."

"I'm counting on that, Damacio. My sister's life is in your hands," Clayton nodded before leaving out.

"My prayers have finally been answered. My son is awake," Karmen said, holding Kasir's hand.

"How long have I been here?" Kasir asked.

"Two weeks although it felt like two lifetimes," she smiled, stroking her son's hand. "Seeing you awake and talking, feels like the happiest day of my life."

"I'm happy to be alive. How's Crystal...is she okay?" Kasir questioned.

"Crystal?" Karmen gave her son a perplexed look. "Who is Crystal?"

"The woman who was with me when the shooting happened. We'd just left the restaurant. I was trying to protect her. Crystal didn't get shot did she?"

"No. You were the only person who got injured. Tell me more about Crystal." Karmen smiled warmly.

"She's a woman I've been seeing. It's a new relationship but..."

"Sorry to interrupt," the nurse said, opening the door. "But we need to run some test on Mr. Collins, so we have to clear his room."

"No problem," Karmen turned to the nurse and said. "I'll be out in the hallway." She told Kasir before kissing him on the forehead.

"Mom, is Kasir okay? Did he take a turn for the worse? I've been trying to call you ever since I got your text but you haven't responded." Clayton was breathing heavily and his face was consumed with fear.

"Calm down. I'm sorry, I put my phone on mute. I didn't mean to worry you. Kasir's awake!" Karmen beamed. "Your brother is going to be just fine." She hugged Clayton tightly.

'Thank God," Clayton closed his eyes and said. "Can I go see him?"

"They're running some test on him right now but

when they're done, you can go see your brother."

"Does dad know about Kasir?"

"I sent him a text. I'm sure he'll be here soon. Did you know a woman named Crystal was with your brother when he got shot?"

His mother switched the subject so quickly, Clayton was caught off guard but played it off with ease. "No, I didn't. Who is she?"

"A woman your brother has been seeing."

"Really...I had no idea Kasir was seeing anyone." Clayton did his best to sound surprised.

"Neither did I. Kasir said he was trying to protect her when he got shot. What I find puzzling, is if she was with your brother when he was shot, why hasn't she been at the hospital to see how he's doing. Have you seen a woman here asking about your brother?"

"No. The only people I've seen at the hospital visiting Kasir, is you and dad."

"You know the woman I told you your father was having an affair with?"

"Yes, what about her?"

"Her name is Crystal too. What sort of sick coincidence is that." Karmen shook her head.

"Crystal isn't an uncommon name," Clayton said, trying to eliminate any suspicions his mother might have.

"True but still."

"Speaking of dad, is everything okay between the two of you? I couldn't help but notice your interaction has been limited, while you're both here at the hospital."

"I wasn't going to mention anything until your sister came home but umm," Karmen paused, as if wanting to choose her words carefully. "There's no easy way to say this but I'm divorcing your father."

"I thought you said you all were working things out."

"That was before I found out your father is still seeing his mistress."

"Are you sure he's seeing her?"

"Positive. A video of them having sex was sent to our house. I'm guessing it was her sick way of letting me know, she's still having an affair with my husband."

"Mom, I'm so sorry," Clayton said, hugging his mother. "I can't believe dad would betray you again, after you were willing to give him another chance. He doesn't deserve you. Know that I'm here for you... whatever you need."

"Thank you, Clayton. But I'll be fine. Now that Kasir is on the road to recovery, I'm just waiting for Ashton to come home and then I'll be filing for divorce."

"You know dad isn't going to make the divorce process easy for you. In his mind, you'll always be his wife."

"You damn right," Allen stated, walking up from behind, startling Karmen and Clayton. "I don't know what your mother has told you but there will be no divorce."

"Clayton, fill your father in on what's going on with Kasir, while I go to the restroom."

"Karmen, you can keep ignoring me all you want but this conversation is far from over," Allen called out, as his wife walked away.

"Dad, keep your voice down. People are staring," Clayton said.

"I don't give a damn about these people. I sit on the board at this hospital. These people can kiss my ass. That's my wife!" he bellowed.

"Not sure if you know but Kasir is awake and alert. They're tending to him now, running some test." Clayton informed his father, refusing to engage in any conversation regarding his mother and the state of their marriage.

"I know. I already spoke to the doctor. All of our praying paid off. We have Kasir back and hopefully soon, he'll be a hundred percent again. But while your mother is in the restroom, I want to speak with you."

"If it's about the divorce, I don't want to get in the middle of that." Clayton made clear.

"As I stated before, there will be no divorce," Allen stated, matter of factly. "But that's not what I want to speak with you about."

"If it isn't about the divorce then what?"

"Damacio. Why were you at his house earlier today?"

Clayton knew it wouldn't be wise to deny something his father knew as fact, so instead he answered his question. "To see if he heard from Ashton and when she was coming home."

"What did he say?"

"He said, hopefully she'll be home by Friday."

"I see," Allen nodded. "Did he say anything else?"

"Besides reassuring me that Ashton was fine, no Damacio didn't say anything else."

"After what they did, I don't understand why you would associate with anyone in the Hernandez family," Allen scoffed.

"Because my sister and your daughter is married to Damacio which technically makes her a member of the Hernandez family too," Clayton reminded his father.

"Don't you dare say something like that again!" Allen spit, pointing his finger directly in Clayton's face. "Ashton is a Collins. Soon she'll realize Damacio doesn't deserve her."

"You mean like, how you don't deserve mother?"

Allen mean mugged his son, as if he was ready to break Clayton's neck with his bare hands. "You've always been very close to your mother, so I'm going to let your comment slide. But watch your mouth. I won't tolerate any disrespect from you."

"If you'll excuse me. They seem to be finished in Kasir's room. I'm going to spend some quality time with my brother," Clayton said, leaving his father standing alone.

Allen clenched his jaw. He tried to contain his anger but with Clayton's dismissive attitude and his wife barely acknowledging his presence, made it difficult. He was used to controlling situations and determining the outcome. For the first time in his life, Allen wasn't sure how to reign his family in but one way or the other, they would fall in line. Either willingly or by force.

Chapter Five

Flip The Switch

"When you asked me to meet you for lunch, at first I was going to decline," Vannette stated, placing the napkin on her lap. "But when you said you were treating and this is one of my favorite restaurants, I decided to hear what you had to say."

"I wanted to apologize for what happened with Clayton," said Brianna, sweetly.

"Now you want to apologize? When I first confronted you about scheming to get my man in bed, you basically told me to get over it. Now you want to apologize."

"First of all, Clayton wasn't yo' man."

"I was dating him. You met Clayton through me. You knew we were seeing each other. If you were any type of friend, that would've made him off limits to you," Vannette snapped.

"You asked me to participate in a threesome with you and him, which meant Clayton was no longer off limits."

"Brianna, you're so full of shit. You all but seduced him. I witnessed you in action. You had already decided, you were gonna get Clayton in bed. I was just dumb enough to lead the way."

"You're right. I was attracted to Clayton the moment you introduced us. I could've turned down the threesome request but I decided to use it, to my advantage."

"I guess I should say thank you for admitting the fuckin' truth," Vannette mocked. "Is that why you invited me here to clear your conscious?"

"No. I don't want a man coming between our friendship. We've known each other for years. It shouldn't end because we both slept with the same guy."

"When you put it like that, I guess you're right," Vannette shrugged, taking a sip of her wine.

"I'm glad you see things my way," Brianna smiled widely. "Now that we've gotten that out the way, what have you been up to?"

"Not too much. Just school and working. What about you?"

"I'm actually in school too for hair and makeup."

"Wow, that's great! You've always wanted to do that."

"Yeah, it was a parting gift from Caesar. I guess you can call it a share of my severance package," Brianna laughed.

"Must be nice. Did he let you keep the car too? I saw it parked outside when I pulled up."

"Yes, and he got me an apartment that's paid up for the year. It's not as luxurious as the house I lived in with him but it's super cute and it allows me to stay here in Houston."

"Lucky you. It seems all is working out in your favor."

"It is. I have no complaints. And how 'bout you? Besides school and work, what else do you have going on in your personal life? Are you still seeing Jeff?" Brianna casually asked.

"We've spoken a few times but I've been busy with school and work, so Jeff hasn't been a priority."

"What about, Clayton...have you spoken to him?"

Vannette stopped eating her Cajun chicken pasta and placed her fork down. "Now it all makes sense."

"What do you mean?"

"You didn't invite me to lunch to save our friendship. You wanted to find out if I've been in contact with Clayton. Let me guess, he's bored with you already,"

Vannette quipped.

"Oh please."

"Oh please my ass. Remember, I know Clayton very well. He has an extremely short attention span when it comes to women. Even the ones who give great head."

"Really Vannette...you mad cause I give better fellatio than you? I thought we were past all the immaturity and we weren't going to let what happened with Clayton come between us."

"I agreed not to let it come between our friendship but I have no intentions of helping you make Clayton your man."

"Why?" Brianna laughed. "Is it because you think you have a chance?" Vannette ignored her friend's question but the answer was written all over her face. "I hate to break it to you but Clayton is way outta your league. You're much too sweet for him."

"You think a conniving chick like you is a better fit for him?"

"Honestly, yes I do." Brianna smiled coyly," sliding her hair behind her ear. "We understand each other."

"To answer your question, yes I've spoken to Clayton. I might not be as seasoned as you but what I've learned is, dogs have a tendency to lay their head, where they feel the most comfortable. That gives me one up on you."

Vannette and Brianna locked eyes. They both wanted the same thing and neither planned on backing down, friendship, pride or self-respect be damned. As far as they were concerned, may the best woman win.

"Breakfast seems a little early today," Ashton comment-ed when Chi brought in her tray of food.

"How can you tell? It's not like there's a clock in here."

"True but you mentioned before dinner was at 6:15pm. Then a few hours later, you bring me a few snacks which somewhat holds me over but normally when you bring my food in the morning, I'm starving. Today I'm not that hungry."

"I can always bring you the food later," Chi said, picking the tray back up.

"No! No!" Ashton yelled, taking the tray back. "My appetite will kick in soon."

"But you're right. I am early today," Chi admitted with a slight grin.

"Is there a reason why?"

"I have to step out for a minute and I wanted to make sure you were fed before I left."

"How considerate of you," Ashton said, taking a bite of her pancakes.

"Believe it or not, I'm not all bad. I told you, I wish you no harm."

"Well, somebody wishes me harm. Why else would I be kept away from my family. You don't seem like a bad person but if there was anything good about you, I don't think you would've abducted me."

"I get why you feel that way but..."

"But what? I wish you would just tell me who is keeping me away from my family and why," Ashton pleaded.

"It's not from your family, it's your husband. Alejo Hernandez hired me to kidnap you," Chi revealed.

"What...why?! He doesn't know me. I've never even met the man."

"From what I understand, there is a lot of bad blood between your family and the Hernandez family. Alejo doesn't want you married to his son. He wanted to put some distance between the two of you."

"So he has you keeping me here in this room! How long does he plan on holding me hostage?"

"I'm not sure. Maybe until he feels his son has moved on."

"Damacio loves me. He won't move on!" Ashton exclaimed.

"Every man moves on at some point, when they can't have the one they love," Chi reasoned. "I have to go," he said, glancing down at his phone. "I'll check on you when I get back."

Ashton was tempted to throw her tray at Chi, when he turned his back to walk away. She was furious he dismissed the bond she felt her and Damacio shared. What made it worst, was Ashton worried he might be right. If she was kept here long enough, would her husband let go and move on.

"I can't think about that right now," she whimpered, picking at her food.

"Look what we have here." A rowdy tone echoed throughout the room. Ashton looked up to match a face to the unfamiliar voice.

"Who are you and why are you in this room with me?" she asked, scooting back against the headboard of the bed. The unsavory looking man instantly made Ashton feel uneasy.

"Chi had to step out and asked me to keep an eye on you. He forgot to mention how pretty you are," the man said, wrapping a piece of Ashton's hair around his finger. "I wanted to make sure you were okay down here."

"I'm fine," Ashton mumbled, flinging the man's hand away.

"Why you being so mean? Pretty girl like you, supposed to be nice and sweet," he said, continuing to play with Ashton's hair. "I bet you taste sweet too."

"Excuse me, I need to use the bathroom." Ashton jumped up from the bed and tried to slide around the menacing figure but he blocked her path.

"Where you think you going?"

"I told you I need to use the bathroom," she repeated nervously.

"The bathroom can wait. Chi ain't gonna be gone long, we don't have much time." The broad-shouldered man gave Ashton a sinister smile.

"I really need to pee!" she blurted, becoming gripped in fear.

"This dick will stop any peeing yo' pretty ass got to do," he barked, grabbing Ashton's arm.

"Get off me!" she yelled. Ashton tried her best to escape the man's grip but he was much too strong.

"Don't fight it. I promise not to beat it up too bad," he chuckled, ripping Ashton's shirt. She reached for the tray and swung it at the man but he caught it and tossed the tray across the room, like it was a piece of paper. He then lifted Ashton up by her neck, throwing her down on the bed like a ragdoll.

"Please don't do this to me!" she begged, trying to crawl away but he pulled Ashton's foot, as she kicked her legs determined to fight him off. But her slim frame was no match for the robust predator.

"I told you I'd be gentle, so calm yo' ass down," he grumbled in Ashton's ear, pinning her body underneath his, while yanking down her shorts and underwear. The smell of his cheap cologne made her want to vomit but all she could taste was the tears streaming down her face.

Ashton continued screaming out for help but it felt like no one could hear her. The walls seemed to be closing in on her and when she glanced down, she caught a glimpse of the man's hardened dick. She tried to close her legs but he used his muscular thighs to pry them back open. Ashton literally wanted to die. She'd made up her mind, after he raped her, she would break the mirror in the bathroom and use a shard of glass to slit her wrist. She refused to relive being violated every day for the rest of her life. Her mind began to drift off, as she accepted her fate.

"Man, what tha fuck is you doin'!" Chi barked, knocking him off Ashton. "Are you fuckin' crazy!" he roared.

As the two men tussled, Ashton raced to the bathroom and locked the door. She bent down, pressing her body against the wall, praying no one would get in and hurt her all over again. She could hear Chi and the man arguing, as Ashton cried her heart out, begging God to save her.

Chapter Six

New Tactics

Allen stood from a distance, watching his wife get out the shower and moisturize her wet body. He was still attracted to Karmen, as much or even more, then the first time he laid eyes on her. He wanted his wife back, not only in his life but in his bed.

"How long have you been standing there?" questioned Karmen, covering her naked body with a towel, when she noticed her husband staring at her with lust in his eyes.

"Not that long. I didn't realize you were taking a

shower. I wanted to speak with you about Ashton," Allen explained.

"Is Ashton back...have you spoken to her?"

"No but I'm very concerned."

"I've been concerned but you tried to convince me I was worrying for no reason and our daughter was fine. What's changed?"

"Clayton went to see Damacio. I'm starting to think maybe he was lying about being in touch with Ashton. That he knows something has happened to her."

"Is that what Clayton told you...did something happen to our daughter?" Karmen's eyes widened with distress.

"I'm not sure but I put my men on it. I don't trust what Damacio said and I refuse to take any chances when it comes to saving our daughter's life."

"I knew something was wrong," Karmen sighed, putting her head down. "I felt it in my gut but I was so consumed with Kasir getting better, I just pushed the uncertainties out of my head. I don't know what I'll do if something happens to my baby girl," she wept.

"I promise, I won't let anything happen to Ashton." Allen reassured his wife, holding her closely. "We'll get through this together, like we always do."

As Brianna left class, she couldn't stop thinking about

the conversation she had with Vannette the other day. She was expecting her somewhat credulous friend, to bow out of a potential nasty love triangle with Clayton, not challenge her to battle for his affection. Brianna never shied away from a competition but she wasn't quite sure how to proceed with Clayton. He'd been distant lately, not even a brief text message. She called him once and left a message but still not a word. Brianna knew she'd be playing herself if she continued to reach out to him, so she decided to try another approach that wouldn't make her seem too desperate but also remind Clayton, what he'd been missing.

Brianna knew the gym Clayton worked out at three times a week and he always went the exact same time, as it was across the street from his family's office building. Luckily there were plenty of restaurants and businesses in the area, so it wouldn't appear stalkerish, if Brianna just so happened to run into her prey. She arrived about thirty minutes before Clayton normally came out, in case he ended his workout early. Brianna sipped on her Caramel Mocha Frappuccino patiently waiting for him to make an appearance.

"Where are you, Clayton?" Brianna mumbled under her breath, checking her makeup on her phone's camera. She dabbed on a little more lip gloss, fluffed out her hair and switched back to man watching. After another fifteen minutes, her target was insight. "Finally!" She grabbed her drink and purse, headed out the door.

Brianna kept her head down, pretending to be texting on her phone, while crossing the street. She wasn't concerned what Clayton was doing because her high waist jeans, low cut bodysuit and open toe heels, would garner his attention without much effort.

"Brianna!" Clayton called out as they were passing each other. She ignored him at first, keeping to her plan of seeming immersed in her phone. She waited for Clayton to call out her name a second time, before capturing his gaze. "I thought that was you. How are you?" he asked, appearing happy to see her.

"I'm really good and you?" she asked politely.

"Decent. I have a lot going on but it's slowing coming together. Going to the gym does help with the stress."

"Is that where you're coming from now?" she questioned, as if not already knowing the answer.

"Yeah, I'm assuming my attire is giving it away. I'm headed to my office now to shower and change. I'm not particularly a fan of public bathrooms," Clayton smiled. "I'm starving. After I change, how about you join me for dinner?"

"I would but I'm actually on my way to meet someone for dinner," Brianna lied. She realized she was taking a gamble declining Clayton's dinner invitation but she was hoping it would pay off in spades. She was well aware, most men were hunters by nature but for a man like Clayton, Brianna had to play the chase game just right.

"Really...well I won't keep you. Maybe another time." Clayton kept his demeanor calm yet pleasant but Brianna knew he wasn't used to women denying his requests.

"Yeah, maybe another time." Brianna gave Clayton a kiss on the cheek, making sure he took in the seductive scent of her perfume, before waving goodbye. *Fuck, this better work!* she thought to herself, feeling Clayton stare her down, as she walked away.

Ashton felt like she had locked herself in the bathroom forever. She was too afraid to open the door and eventually fell asleep. It wasn't until what sounded like a stampede of horses coming down the stairs, did she wake up. She turned off the bathroom light and tried to remain quiet as possible but worried the sound of her racing heartbeat, could be heard through the door.

With all the commotion in the bedroom, Ashton assumed Chi and the man who tried to rape her, had come back. She pressed her ear against the door and could hear footsteps getting closer and closer. *Please make them go away...please,* she prayed to herself. When someone started knocking, she cringed. *That sick bastard is fuckin' with me. He's trying to taunt me before he kicks the door in,* Ashton closed her eyes and cried.

"Is someone in there?" a deep toned male voice

asked, before fidgeting with the doorknob. Ashton remained silent. His voice was unfamiliar but nonthreatening. "Ashton Collins, are you in there? If so, it's okay to come out. Your father sent us."

Ashton hesitated but only for a moment. She knew it had to be real. Her father saved her, like he always did. When she opened the door, there were at least six men, all carrying assault weapons.

"Please take me home to my family." Ashton told the man, ready to put this nightmare behind her.

Chapter Seven

Game Changer

Crystal was getting dressed, preparing to go visit Kasir at the hospital. Like she figured, Clayton never called to give her an update regarding his brother. But her bestie Remi, stayed true to the cause and became friendly with one of the nurses at the hospital. When she got word Kasir was awake and able to have visitors other than immediate family, Crystal was willing to risk it all to go see him. She put on a free falling cashmere, off the shoulder, hunter green dress with matching heels. As she debated which purse would complement her look the best, Crystal heard a knock at the door.

"I bet that's Remi," Crystal said out loud, while heading to the door.

"With the expression on your face, I'm positive you weren't expecting to see me. May I come in?" Crystal stood in the entryway speechless. "I'm assuming that's a yes," said Karmen, walking past a stunned Crystal.

"How did you find out where I live?" Crystal spoke up and asked, once the element of surprise wore off.

"By using the same private investigator who informed me you were having an affair with my husband."

"I'm so sorry, but so you know, that affair is over."

"Did the affair end before or after you had your sex tape sent to my house?"

"I swear, I had no idea that tape was going to be sent to you," Crystal implored.

"No need to lie. Honestly, I'm glad you sent me the tape. It was the sort of ammunition I needed, to finally walk away from my marriage. But that's not the reason I'm here."

"If it isn't about your husband then what?"

"My son Kasir," Karmen said, placing her purse down on the table before approaching Crystal.

Crystal was tempted to fix her mouth and start lying but she wasn't sure what Karmen knew. Plus, she had that same intimidating aura as her husband, which made her want to stay mute. Mrs. Collins didn't just look rich, rich, rich, she exuded wealth, class and sophistication. From the puffed shoulder fluid crepe jumpsuit, cinched with a wrap style waist tie and cut with subtly tapered legs, to the pointy toe pumps, featuring chain hardware at the vamp and a towering mirrored heel, the woman oozed effortless style with grace. Even Karmen's diamonds were simple but screamed, I cost a fortune. It was all too much for Crystal.

"I see you don't really talk a lot," Karmen commented, when Crystal remained silent, just standing aimlessly.

"I guess I'm still in shock over you being here."

"Well get over it," Karmen advised, moving even closer to Crystal. There was now only a small space between the two women. "When my son woke up, he asked how Crystal was doing. He said this Crystal person, he'd been dating, was with him when he got shot and he was trying to protect her. I thought to myself, how ironic is it that the woman my son is seeing and my husband's mistress, are both named Crystal," she gave a slight sarcastic giggle. "I don't believe in coincidences do you?"

"I guess it depends on the situation," Crystal shrugged.

"Clearly, you have a limited thought process, so we'll narrow the scope of our discussion to this one particular coincidence. Is there two different Crystals, or are you fuckin' my husband and my son?"

Crystal glanced down at the floor and let out a deep sigh. "I only recently found out they were related."

"I believe you."

"You do?" Crystal sounded shocked.

"It would be beyond vile to stoop so low. So yes, I believe you but it doesn't matter because it ends today. I have no problem with you continuing your relationship, with my soon to be ex-husband but Kasir is off limits."

"I can't do that. I lo…"

"Don't you dare use that word!" Karmen put her hand up before Crystal could finish her sentence. "You don't love Kasir and he can't possibly love you."

"That's not true." Crystal shook her head in denial.

"Oh yes it is. Kasir doesn't even know what type of woman you are because the son I raised, would never fuck behind his father."

"It wasn't like that!" Crystal wailed. She was on the verge of spilling the truth. To tell the woman standing in front of her, that she'd been nothing more than a puppet, hired by her other son, to ruin her marriage. Seducing Allen Collins was a job but Kasir had her heart.

"Save your tears," Karmen said, unmoved by Crystal's weeping. "I'm going to give you two options. Take this check I'm prepared to write. It will be more than enough for you to find a new place to live, of course without a forwarding address and change your phone number. You are to have no contact with my son."

"Or?" Crystal waited to hear option number two.

"Or, get ready for the war of your life. Be aware,

I only partake in battles, I'm guaranteed to win. You choose. Which one will it be?"

Karmen and Crystal scrutinized one another with contempt in their eyes. Both pondering what the other was prepared to do, to get what they want. The women shared absolutely nothing in common, except for the men in their lives and that would continue to link them, in more ways than one.

"Daddy, I was so scared I would never see you again!" Ashton sobbed, falling into her father's arms.

"It's okay, you're home now," Allen said, hugging his daughter tightly. Even with her father's strong arms wrapped around her, Ashton was shaking uncontrollably.

Throughout the duration of the car ride, to arriving at her parent's estate, Ashton couldn't stop her body from trembling. She believed or at least hoped, once she felt secure, it would stop but it didn't. Allen slowly walked his daughter over to the couch, so she could sit down. She laid her head on his shoulder not saying a word but the tears that continued to flow, spoke for her.

"You have no idea how horrible it was. I thought I was going to die," Ashton said, between cries. "And I would be dead if you hadn't saved me." She squeezed her father's arm, having flashbacks of fighting to keep from being raped and escaping to the bathroom, thinking she'd die there. Ashton couldn't stop reliving the nightmare and wondered if she would ever feel safe again.

When she heard the doorbell ring, Ashton immediately jumped. "It's okay, sweetheart. It's probably your brother. He must've forgotten his key," Allen said, seeing how visibly shaken his daughter was. "I'll be right back."

As Allen headed to the door, he glanced back and saw Ashton huddling on the couch, rocking back and forth. It broke his heart to see his youngest child completely traumatized. He wasn't sure what he could do to make things right for her again. *Hopefully seeing her brother, will help put Ashton at ease,* Allen thought to himself as he opened the door.

"Hello, Allen. Is my wife here?"

"What the hell are you doing showing up at my home?!" he barked, stepping forward.

"I came to see Ashton."

"She's not here and you have some nerves showing your face at my door."

"I didn't come here to fight with you, Allen. I came for my wife. Now can you let me in?" Damacio asked, remaining civil.

"Hell no! I told you she wasn't here...now go!" Allen demanded.

"I know Ashton is here, or will be shortly. If necessary, I'll wait in my car, until she arrives." Damacio wasn't backing down.

"You listen to me," Allen scoffed, stepping outside, closing the door behind him. "You get off my property and don't you ever show your face around here again!" he warned through clenched teeth.

"If you think I'm leaving here without seeing…"

"Daddy, what's going on out here?" Ashton asked, before seeing her husband. "Damacio!" She ran over to him, melting in his arms.

"My baby. It's so good to hold you again." Damacio didn't want to let his wife go. Feeling Ashton's body against his, was something he believed would never happen again.

"Ashton, you should come back inside and Damacio needs to go." Allen stated, putting his hand around his daughter's arm.

"The only place Ashton is going, is home with me." Damacio shot back, locking eyes with the man he once had a close relationship with.

"Daddy please!" Ashton put her hand up, stopping him from getting in Damacio's face. "Can you give us a moment alone?"

"I don't think that's a good idea. You've been through a lot. You should come back inside and get some much needed rest," Allen suggested.

"I need to speak to Damacio, alone…please, daddy."

"I'll be inside." Allen said, grudgingly.

Ashton held onto Damacio's hand tightly, waiting for her father to close the door, so they could have some privacy. "I'm sorry about my dad."

"You don't have to apologize for your father. I don't want to talk about him anyway. How are you?" Damacio pulled Ashton back in his arms. "Baby, I just wanna take you home."

"I want to stay here tonight."

"Why? You need to be home with me...your husband."

"Damacio, these last few weeks have been a nightmare. Tonight, I just need to rest my head someplace where I feel safe."

"You don't feel safe with me?"

Ashton had her head down, not answering her husband's question. Damacio placed his hand underneath her chin and lifted it up. He saw the sadness in her eyes. She appeared depleted.

"It was your father."

"What about my father?" Damacio questioned.

"He's the one who had me abducted. That's how desperate your father is to keep us apart."

"Ashton, are you sure?"

"Yes! Chi, the man your father hired, he told me. I'm sure he figured, I would never live long enough to ever tell you or anyone else the truth."

"Baby, I'm so, so sorry," Damacio said, wiping the tears from her cheek. I knew my father was ruthless but never did I believe he would try to hurt me this deeply."

"He wasn't trying to hurt you, he wanted to hurt me."

"Ashton, I love you. You're my wife. If you hurt, then I hurt too. He pulled his wife close to his chest. "I promise. My father will be dealt with. I put that on everything but I still want you home with me."

"I want to be home with you too but not tonight. I haven't even seen my mother yet. Don't be mad."

"I'm not. How can I be mad after everything you've been through," Damacio said, stroking her hair. "I understand. You stay here tonight and I'll bring you home tomorrow." He kissed Ashton on her forehead. "Just know I love you more than anything."

"I love you too. I want to go lay down but I'll call you later on tonight." Ashton hugged and kissed Damacio one last time before going back inside. "Dad, were you standing there the entire time?" she asked, closing the door.

"Yes. I wanted to make sure you weren't harmed in any way," Allen said, staring out the window, watching as Damacio drove away.

"My husband would never hurt me."

"How can you be so sure, especially after what his father did."

"You were listening to our conversation. How could you?"

"I'm your father and I will always do whatever I deem necessary to protect you. "

"I don't need protection from Damacio."

"Maybe but he wasn't able to protect you from his father. Damacio knows how dangerous Alejo is. He should've been more proactive. If he had, none of this would've happened to you."

Ashton turned away, thinking about what her father said. His words resonated with her. She didn't admit it to Damacio but she was too scared to go back home. She worried his father would try and harm her again and Ashton knew, she couldn't survive another nightmare like that.

"Daddy, I really want to go upstairs and get some rest. We can finish talking about this later."

"Okay baby girl. I only want what's best for you."

"I know," she nodded walking up the spiral staircase."

Allen went to make himself a drink and sat down in his study. He needed to take the edge off. Between Kasir being in the hospital, Ashton completely traumatized and feeling his wife slipping away, the patriarch of the Collins family, was at a crossroads.

"Dad, I got here as soon as I could," Clayton said, entering the study. His father was sitting in a plush leather chair, behind the desk with his back facing the door. "Where's Ashton?"

"Your sister's upstairs resting," Allen turned around in his chair and said.

"I'm not used to seeing you drink in the middle of the day," Clayton commented, noticing his father had a glass of liquor in his hand, with a bottle next to him. "How's Ashton holding up?"

"I have a lot on my mind and Ashton's doing okay.

She's home now, which is the most important thing," he said pouring himself another drink. "Damacio left here not too long ago but I'm sure you already knew that." Allen eyed his son indignantly.

"I did call Damacio after we got off the phone. He's her husband. I felt he had the right to know."

"I don't give a damn what you think you know. That man isn't welcome here. The Hernandez family is dead to us. Every last one of them!" Allen shouted, slamming his glass down on top of the desk.

"Is Ashton aware of this because from my understanding her last name is Hernandez too. Is she not welcomed here either?"

"Boy, don't play with me," Allen seethed. "I'm doing everything I can to keep this family together and I don't need any shit talking from you."

"If that's true, then I suggest you learn to accept Damacio is Ashton's husband."

"I doubt they'll be married for much longer. Alejo was the one responsible for your sister's kidnapping."

"What! How do you know this?"

"I overheard Ashton tell Damacio. He wanted her to come home with him but she wanted to stay here with us...her family."

"That sonofabitch! It sounds like some sick shit Alejo would do." Clayton shook his head, furious as what he'd just learned. "Damn, I wish those Haitians would've killed him when they had the chance," he fumed, biting down on his lip.

"Me too but Alejo will get his. I'm not done with that man. Now, do you understand why I don't want your sister anywhere near Damacio?"

"I do but..."

"But nothing!" Allen roared, cutting Clayton off. "Here in this house, is where Ashton belongs. Damacio isn't the right man for her. The sooner we help her accept that, the better off she'll be. I need you to support me on this son, instead of having secret meetings with Damacio. He's the enemy!"

"It wasn't secret meetings. We were working together to bring Ashton home," Clayton explained. "I don't like the Hernandez family either but I have to admit, I do believe Damacio loves my sister very much."

"I don't give a damn and neither should you. Damacio doesn't love her as much as we do and we can protect her. So, is your loyalty to this family or Damacio?"

"Of course it's to this family."

"Then start acting like it!" Allen stood up from his chair and demanded. Pounding his fist down. "Help me make sure your sister stays here, with me and your mother, where she'll be safe. Remember Clayton, family sticks together."

Clayton was torn. He saw firsthand how happy Ashton was with Damacio. He was the first man who was able to tame his venturesome sister. To keep them apart almost seemed cruel. Under normal circumstances, Clayton wouldn't have a problem with that but knowing they were genuinely in love, gave him pause.

Still, finding out Alejo was responsible for Ashton's kidnapping, was a game changer. It would weigh heavily on whatever decision Clayton made.

Chapter Eight

Quench The Flame

"Thank you for meeting me on such short notice," Gustaf said, when Caesar sat down. They met at a bar in Baytown, a smaller city outside of Houston.

"Not a problem. Alejo gave me a heads up to be expecting your call. He asked me to assist you anyway I can. Tell me what do you need."

"As you know, Alejo is having problems with Allen Collins. The men I hired to take care of the problem, missed their mark." Gustaf stated.

"So, his son Kasir getting shot, was simply a causality?" Caesar inquired.

"Yes it was."

"I had no idea you were responsible for the shooting. That was a major fuck up. Kasir almost died."

"You sound like you're taking it personally." Gustaf glared at Caesar with a raised eyebrow.

"I don't like dealing wit' messy muthafuckers."

"Neither do I. That's why the men I hired are dead," he divulged.

"I ain't say you needed to do all that." Caesar raised his shoulder with indifference.

"They left me no choice. Somehow, the police were able to link the shooting to them. It was only a matter of time before they were caught and brought in for questioning. I couldn't take the chance of anything leading back to my boss."

"Of course you couldn't. Alejo would then have to kill you." Caesar nodded.

"That's correct," Gustaf acknowledged. "I don't have any more men here that I trust to finish the job. I could bring in some men from Mexico but with everything going on with the border situation, it could take a while. As I'm sure you know by now, Alejo isn't a very patient man, which doesn't leave me with a lot of time."

"I'm assuming that's where I come in?" Caesar leaned forward, waiting for Gustaf's reply to the question he already knew the answer to.

"Yes. I need for you to introduce me to some men,

who can eliminate Alejo's problem permanently. Will you help me?"

"I'll help you but only under one condition."

"Which is?"

"Allen Collins is our only target. The rest of his family members are off limits. Are we clear on that?"

"We're clear," Gustaf agreed.

"Then we good."

"Excellent." Gustaf extended his hand over the table and the two men shook on their newly formed alliance.

"Girl, you move around more than someone in witness protection," Remi cracked as she was helping Crystal unpack.

"You ain't lying. I'm so tired of packing and unpacking. Can a bitch just stay put for a year," Crystal complained. "This shit is crazy."

"I still can't believe you took the money," Remi smacked, putting the last bowl in the kitchen cabinet.

"Did I really have a fuckin' choice!" Crystal popped back.

"You could've told the head bitch in charge, hell no! Talk about bold. She ran you out yo' own crib. Got you relocating like you out here on the run."

"Trust me, once I got over feeling intimidated by

that ice queen, I was tempted to tell Karmen Collins to fuck herself."

"What stopped you?" Remi wanted to know.

"Kasir. What's the point of going to battle with that woman, if I'll lose Kasir anyway. There's no way he'll want me, once he finds out about my relationship with his father," Crystal rationalized. "It made more sense to take the money and disappear out his life. I rather him wonder what happened then know the truth and hate me."

"I feel you but the two of you will meet again. I mean, yeah you did move to the other side of town but ain't so many places you can go in Houston."

"Please, Kasir and I don't run in the same circles. It was a crazy coincidence we met in the first place. I have you to thank for that," Crystal winked. "Plus, by the time we meet again, as you put it. I'm sure he would've moved on and found a woman that's more his type."

"And what type would that be?" Remi wondered.

"You know, classy and sophisticated like his mother. I bet that woman wakes up looking like money. She oozes champagne and caviar dreams," Crystal laughed. "Talk about being polar opposites."

"Have you ever considered maybe that's why Kasir likes you?" Remi reasoned. "They do say opposites attract. Maybe he doesn't want someone like his mother. She sounds like a hard act to follow anyway. It would be draining trying to find a woman who measures up to his mother. Especially since he's probably put her on a pedestal his entire life."

"I never thought about that," Crystal said, putting down a towel she was folding. "Kasir did meet me in all my hoochie glory," she joked. "His dad met the fake me. Pretending to be a bootleg version of his wife. But Kasir knows the real me," she smiled.

"Yep," Remi nodded in agreement. "Everyone doesn't want the polished princess. Some men can appreciate an around the way girl."

"None of that matters now," she shrugged. "I took the money and it's time for me to live my life, knowing Kasir won't be a part of it. I guess there's no Julia Roberts, Pretty Woman fairytale ending for me," Crystal said sadly.

"Good morning! Look what I brought you," Karmen beamed holding up a white paper bag. "Those waffle breakfast tacos you love so much."

"Wow! You made my day," Kasir smiled," hanging up the phone. "I wasn't looking forward to eating any of that bland food this morning," he continued, sitting upright in his hospital bed.

"Well, I'm happy I made your day," Karmen said, handing Kasir the bag. "Ashton wanted to come but we thought it'd be better for her to stay home and get some much needed rest. She sends her love though."

"Yeah, she called me last night. I could tell she wasn't up to coming to the hospital. I'm just glad she's home. But Ashton's tough. She'll get through this and come out stronger than ever."

"I agree. So, who were you on the phone with this early in the morning, when I walked in? I hope you're not trying to conduct business from your hospital bed," Karmen remarked, sitting down in the chair near Kasir's bed.

"No, I wasn't conducting business, although I'm anxious to leave this hospital and get back to work. But umm, I was calling the woman I told you about."

"What woman?" Karmen pretended not to know who her son was speaking of.

"The woman who was with me when I got shot... Crystal."

"Oh yes, now I remember you mentioning her. How's she doing?" Karmen asked, like she actually cared but in a way she did. She wanted to know if Crystal was honoring their arrangement.

"I don't know. I haven't been able to get in touch with her. Her cell and home phone have both been disconnected. What if something happened to her." Kasir wondered out loud, sounding worried.

"Kasir, don't get yourself worked up. I'm sure your friend is fine," she said dismissively.

"Mother, she's more than a friend. I care about her deeply. I want to make sure Crystal is okay."

"I apologize." Karmen reached over and gently

touched her son's hand. "I didn't realize you all were so close. "Is there anything I can do?"

Karmen saw her son's eyes light up. His sad expression now had a hint of hope. She wasn't sure what Kasir would say next but whatever it was, Karmen knew she wouldn't approve.

"Will you stop by her apartment and make sure she's okay. For her not to come to the hospital and see me, now her phones are disconnected...that's not like Crystal."

"Kasir, how well do you know this woman? Didn't you say your relationship is relatively new?"

"It is but we've become close after..." Kasir's voice trailed off.

"After what? Kasir, you know you can tell me anything."

"After we took a break. When we first started seeing each other, I had to cut things off," he divulged.

"Why?"

"Because she was involved with a married man. I didn't want any part of it.."

"Of course you didn't. You deserve better than that."

"When I found out about the married man, I let Crystal go. She eventually ended their relationship. That's not exactly true. She said they mutually agreed to end things. He wanted to make things right with his wife and Crystal wanted to see if things could work between us."

"Son, don't take this the wrong way but have you considered that maybe Crystal decided to go back to the married man?"

"Mother, I'm not stupid. Of course I have."

"In no way do I think you're stupid. But it's easy to let our emotions blind us from the truth."

"Sounds like you're speaking from experience." Kasir looked over at his mother, recalling what Clayton had told him a few months ago about their father having an affair.

"I am. Your father and I share three beautiful children together," Karmen smiled sweetly. "We've been married for over twenty years. That's a lot of history but yet I'm able to see the truth. What's your excuse for looking at your relationship with this Crystal woman, through rose colored glasses?"

Kasir glanced up, caught off guard by his mother's question. "I don't have one."

"Good because I know you're smarter than that. But son, I'll be more than happy to go check on your friend if you like."

"That won't be necessary, mother. Crystal has my number and knows where I live. If she wants to get in touch with me, she will. I really do appreciate you offering though and listening to me without being judgmental but also telling me the truth," Kasir smiled.

"You're my son and I love you unconditionally. Don't you ever forget that." She stood up and kissed Kasir on the side of his face. Karmen would do anything to protect her children and she believed getting rid of Crystal, was vital because the woman was poison to her son.

Chapter Nine

The Games We Play

Ashton was lying in bed, staring up at the vintage chandelier, counting the richly hued pink glass drops and clear crystals, seeing which one there were more of. It was just another diversion, to keep her mind off things she wanted to forget. When she was about to start the process all over again, she noticed Damacio was calling her. Instead of pressing decline, like she'd done previously, Ashton hit accept.

"Hello."

"You finally decided to answer my call."

"Sorry. I was sleeping and just woke up," Ashton lied.

"Really, you were still sleeping at three thirty in the afternoon?" Damacio asked.

"Yeah. I had a difficult time falling asleep last night, so I took some sleeping pills this morning."

"Maybe you're having a hard time sleeping because you're supposed to be home with me in our bed."

Ashton rolled over on her stomach and put her head down in the pillow. She immediately regretted taking her husband's call. This was a conversation she was trying to avoid.

"Ashton, do you hear me talking to you?" Damacio called out, after she remained silent.

"No, I accidentally dropped my phone." The lies kept coming.

"It's been over two weeks. When are you coming home?" Damacio wanted to know.

"Soon. I just need a little more time."

"First, you told me it would be one night, then it turned into three. Now it's been over two weeks. This can't continue."

"Be patient."

"What do you think I've been doing!" he barked. "Staying at your parent's house isn't going to make you feel any better."

"But it does make me feel safe!" Ashton barked back.

"I told you, I spoke to my father."

"Yeah and he denied having anything to do with my kidnapping but what did you expect him to say. Like he would ever admit to anything. He's a liar and there's no telling what he's capable of doing!" she fumed.

"So you're just going to stay gone and never come home! You're my wife!" Damacio yelled in frustration. When he was furious, his Spanish accent became thick and he spoke with such rapid speed, Ashton could barely comprehend what he was saying.

"That's not what I said, Damacio."

"You're not fuckin' saying anything!"

"Would you please stop yelling," she uttered. "Listen, let me call you back," Ashton said, hearing a knock at her bedroom door.

"Why?"

"I told you I just woke up. I need to use the restroom. I'll call you back," she said, hanging up before Damacio could say another word. Ashton got up and opened the door. She was happy to see her mother standing there.

"It's beautiful outside. Much too sunny for you to stay cooped up in your room all day." Karmen spoke warmly. "I was thinking we could have lunch by the pool. I can have Bernice cook all your favorites. What do you say." She rubbed Ashton's arm, hoping her daughter would say yes.

"That actually sounds nice. Give me a minute and I'll meet you outside."

"Sounds good. I'll see you shortly." Karmen hugged

her daughter and kissed her on the cheek. She was extremely worried about Ashton. Since coming home, she hadn't been the same. Karmen prayed, getting her out the house, even if it was only by the pool, would get her daughter to open up about what happened during her abduction.

When Clayton arrived at the St. Regis Hotel, he went directly to The Remington, an elegant bar/restaurant that served modern American cuisine and cocktails. It was no surprise when he noticed Jeevan at one of the larger tables, filled with food, liquor and numerous women.

"Are we having a business meeting or a party," Clayton remarked with a sly smile, when he approached Jeevan's table.

"If it isn't the man of the hour!" Jeevan put down his napkin and stood up to shake Clayton's hand. "I was just having a little fun as I waited for your arrival. Please, sit down and join us."

The bevy of beauties who seemed to represent an array of women from Brazil to Africa, smiled widely, welcoming another man joining the table. The ladies were all different shades, shapes and sizes. Their only common denominator, was being easy on the eyes. Clayton's Indian drug connect definitely didn't discriminate, he simply loved the company of beautiful women.

"Please, eat something. I ordered everything off the menu," Jeevan said with glee, biting down on a succulent piece of lamb. He loved to eat, which was obvious based on his heavyset frame. Jeevan seemed to be happiest, when devouring his favorite foods.

"I'm good. I will have a drink though."

Before Clayton could even reach for a bottle, one of the women immediately poured Clayton a glass of champagne.

"It's my pleasure to serve you," the beauty beamed.

"Thank you," he replied smoothly. Clayton also enjoyed the company of beautiful women but he found it inconvenient when he had business on his mind. "We have some things we need to discuss," he reminded Jeevan, who was clearly getting sidetracked.

"Yes! Yes! I know. All business with you, Clayton. Ladies, can you please excuse us. Go sit at another table. Take some bottles with you." Jeevan was very dismissive but the women didn't seem to mind as they quickly scattered away. "Come...sit near me," he waved his hand at Clayton. "I must say, I thought you no longer wanted to continue our arrangement, after I didn't hear from you for a while."

"My apologies. My family has been dealing with a lot, these last few weeks. Finally, things are turning around. For one, my brother is being released from the hospital at the end of the week." You could see the relief on Clayton's face.

"I'm glad to hear that. It's not easy to focus on business when you're dealing with family issues."

"Very true," Clayton agreed.

"With my father's position in our country, the family is never without issues," Jeevan chuckled.

"I can only imagine." Clayton nodded, since Jeevan's father's business was described as the Goldman Sachs of organized crime. He figured dealing with family issues, came with the territory of being one of the biggest Indian crime bosses. "But it's all good now. I'm ready to get back to work."

"Wonderful. I like doing business with you, Clayton. You always conduct yourself very professionally. That's not always the case in this line of work."

"My father constantly reminded me, it's not what you do but how you do it. I plan on being exceedingly successful at this for a very long time, so professionalism is key, plus having the right connect."

"That's where I come in of course," Jeevan grinned proudly.

"Yes and I'm jumping right back in, going even harder. I have a new buyer based in Louisiana who wants to purchase a lot of weight. I keep expanding like this, you'll be moving a ton of product. Can you handle it?" Clayton asked.

"You like making jokes," Jeevan laughed, nudging Clayton's shoulder. "The better you do, the better I do. So expand...expand...expand," he cheered.

"As long as we're on the same page. I have big plans but I need you to keep the product flowing."

"Have I let you down yet?"

"No you haven't and let's keep it that way."

"I shall. Listen, I'm only in town for a few more days. Let's go out and celebrate getting our business booming together." Jeevan did a little wiggle in his chair, being extra jovial.

"Maybe next time you come."

"Oh no, you can't decline my invitation. That would be rude. You wouldn't be rude to the man who is going to make you so much money," he stated playfully, yet his steel stare made it clear, Jeevan was serious.

"Of course I wouldn't."

"Good!" Jeevan slammed his hand down on the table. "First, we'll have a big dinner and then we dance. You bring a date, or you can borrow one of my women for the evening,"

"I appreciate the offer but I have a lady friend I can bring."

"I'm sure you do. A handsome man like yourself, must have an endless supply of women," he winked. "We're going to have a good time. So you know, I can party all night," Jeevan boasted, before continuing to eat the rest of his food.

Partying with Jeevan had zero appeal for Clayton. They shared no mutual interests, besides their love of money and power but he knew it'd be wise to accept Jeevan's invite. It was all part of playing the game.

Clayton witnessed it firsthand with his own father. Once Allen Collins became consumed with white collar visions, he started to hobnob with the corporate elite. He'd have his wife throw elaborate dinner parties at their estate. Soon, Allen became one of them and quickly learned they were more ruthless than any of the rats and wolves he dealt with while building his drug empire. Now Clayton had his own vision and Jeevan would be critical in bringing it to fruition. If dinner, drinks and dancing, would stroke his supplier's ego and build a stronger business relationship, then so be it. Only thing left for Clayton to decide, was which of his women would accompany him tonight.

"You were right. It's so beautiful out here. This is really nice," Ashton gushed, on the unseasonably warm day. "I needed this."

"I knew it and so did I. But I'm glad we're enjoying this time together," Karmen said, lowering her sunglasses. "It's great seeing you smile again. I've missed it."

"Yeah. It's the first time in weeks I haven't thought about the kidnapping. I wish I could erase it from my mind forever," Ashton acknowledged sadly.

"You never told me what happened during that time. It might help to talk about it," Karmen hinted.

"There's nothing to talk about. I was kidnapped. End of story." Ashton shrugged.

"Okay. If you ever change your mind, I'm here or if you don't feel comfortable talking to me about it, you can always see a professional."

"I'm fine." Ashton sounded defensive. Karmen decided not to push and have her daughter completely shut her out.

"So, how is Damacio doing? I'm sure he's ready for you to come home." Karmen hoped changing the subject and bringing up the man Ashton loved, would put a smile back on her daughter's face but she was wrong.

"Things aren't good. He's pressuring me to come home but he doesn't understand I don't feel safe there. His father is the reason that horrible thing happened to me."

"When you say horrible thing, you mean the kidnapping?"

"Yes!" Ashton snapped, although Karmen felt there was more to it but her daughter was holding back.

"What Alejo did was horrible and I'm sure Damacio is furious with him but..."

"No he's not!" Ashton cut her mother off. "His father is denying having anything to do with it and although Damacio won't admit it, I think he believes him. It's so frustrating," she fumed. "I love my husband and I miss him so much but how can I stay married to a man, whose father hates me that much."

"Alejo doesn't hate you, Ashton."

"How can you say that after what he did?" she turned to her mother and asked.

"Trust me, I'm furious. If I knew where Alejo was I would go see him myself. I know he can be ruthless but at one time, I considered him to be a friend. For him to kidnap my daughter is reprehensible, even if he's on the outs with your father. But Alejo doesn't hate you, if anything he hates Allen. It still doesn't excuse what he did. But don't let what he did ruin your marriage. I know how much you love Damacio."

"I do but I need time and Damacio doesn't want to give it to me. Thank goodness I have you and dad. Being here, in this house with the two of you, makes me feel safe and secure. I'm so lucky my parents are still together. I didn't realize how much that mattered to me until now," Ashton admitted.

While they were alone, sitting outside by the pool, Karmen planned on breaking the news to her daughter, that she was filing for divorce. Now that Kasir was about to be released from the hospital, she felt the worst was behind them and the family could move forward. But after what Ashton just said, Karmen had a change of heart. Her daughter was more fragile than she realized and didn't think she could handle finding out her parents were divorcing.

"Your father and I both love you so much. Don't worry about Damacio, he'll come around. Just focus on feeling better."

"I agree, that's why I think I'll go out with Lizzie

and Vannette tonight."

"Lizzie's in town?"

"Yeah, she came home from school for a few days. She called me earlier wanting to hang out but I wasn't in the mood. Now, after my fabulous mother got me outside, basking in this sun, I feel rejuvenated!" Ashton beamed. "I'm ready for a girl's night out."

"I think that's a marvelous idea."

"Me too!" Ashton stood up from the lounge chair. "I love you so much," she said, giving her mother a hug. "You really are the best. Now let me go upstairs and call the girls. Let them know we're going out tonight, to have some fun!"

Karmen smiled with delight, watching her daughter hurry into the house. For the first time since coming back home, she saw a glimpse of that sparkle in Ashton's eyes, she missed so much. If staying married to Allen and them living under the same roof for a little while longer would help her daughter heal, it'd be worth the sacrifice to continue the charade.

Chapter Ten

Party Crashers

"Bitch, you look fuckin' good!" Brianna cooed in the mirror, admiring herself. She was wearing a black mesh dress, with long sleeves, a deep v neck and a slit in the front. The built in panty and snap button closure, gave her attire a hint of trashy to balance out the classy, which was the look she was going for. "Clayton will be ready to lick me down, when he sees me in this," she bragged out loud, while putting the finishing touches on her makeup.

Brianna had resigned herself to a night of Netflix and takeout, when she received an unexpected call from Clayton. Her initial reaction was to play hard to get and hit decline but she remembered how well that didn't work out for her last time and quickly answered.

"Hello." Brianna did her best to sound unbothered.

"Hey, it's me, Clayton. Did I catch you at a bad time?"

"Oh hi, Clayton. No, I was just about to take a shower. I had a long day."

"Do you mind making it a little longer. I was hoping you could join me for dinner."

"Join you for dinner...why are you cooking?"

"Maybe I should've worded that differently. Go out to dinner with me?"

"Sure, I can do that. Is this a casual dinner or..."

"No, not casual at all and we'll be joined by a gentleman I'm doing some business with."

"So, a conservative, uptight, type dinner? I'm only asking, so I know what I should wear," Brianna explained.

"Put on something sexy, that'll make me want to skip dinner and go straight to dessert."

"I can do that."

"Prove it and oh, afterwards we're going dancing. I'll call you when I'm on the way," Clayton said, right before hanging up.

Brianna screamed with excitement when she got off the phone with Clayton. This was the opportunity she had been waiting for and planned to make the most of it. Hence the reason, she pulled out the sexiest dress she owned. Brianna had been saving it for the perfect occasion and seducing Clayton was it.

"He may not know it yet but after tonight, Clayton Collins will be my man," Brianna vowed, blowing herself a kiss in the mirror, to seal the deal.

"Girl, you been checking your phone all fuckin' night. What is up with you?" Ashton questioned Vannette as she sipped on her third glass of champagne.

"Clayton called me earlier but I didn't have my phone. Like an hour or so later, I tried calling him back but he didn't answer. I even sent him a text but he hasn't responded."

"This is supposed to be a girl's night out. Who cares what my brother is doing. I thought you were done with him anyway," Ashton scoffed, filling Lizzie's glass back up with champagne.

"It's not that easy," Vannette shrugged. "I'm not ready to give up on Clayton yet."

"Whatever works for you, love. But can we not talk about my messy brother tonight. We're supposed to be partying."

"Yeah we are but this lounge is sorta dead," Lizzie commented looking around.

"I agree but I haven't been out in so long, I have no clue what's poppin' tonight," Ashton sighed.

"There's this new club that just opened called Cyclone. I heard it's kinda hot," Vannette mentioned, while eyeing her phone.

"What the fuck are we waiting for! Let's go ladies!" Ashton announced, gulping down the last of her champagne, ready to hit the next spot.

The women arrived at Cyclone rather quickly, since it was literally down the street. There was a long line around the building but luckily, Vannette knew one of the bouncers, who was posted out front and he let the ladies right in.

"Now this is what I'm talking about! Let the fun begin!" Ashton cheered, looking around for the nearest bar.

"Wait!" Lizzie called out, grabbing Ashton's arm as she was walking off. "Let's go to the ladies room and do a little more of that candy I gave you before we hit the bar."

"How about we get a table first and get that bottle service poppin', then we can go powder our noses," Ashton laughed.

"Cool!" Lizzie smiled.

"Where did Vannette go?" Ashton asked, realizing her friend had disappeared.

"I'm not sure," Lizzie said, glancing around.

"You go look for Vannette and I'ma go talk to the waitress over there about getting us a table and bottle service."

"Sounds good. BRB," Lizzie winked, as she went off to find Vannette.

Ashton was making her way over to a waitress, who was standing near a roped off area, that seemed to be one of the VIP sections. As she got closer, her eyes zoomed in on a very familiar face. Ashton damn near knocked the waitress over, trying to get to her man.

"What the fuck are you doing?!" she screamed at Damacio. He was sitting much too closely to another woman, who was being very touchy, feely with her husband. Security had ran up on the scene before Damacio even had a chance to respond. He put his hand up, letting them know to back down, that he had the situation under control.

"Who is she?" the woman leaned in and asked Damacio.

"I'm his fuckin' wife!" Ashton flashed her massive rock, holding her hand steady for all to see.

"I didn't know," the woman snarled.

"You knew he was fuckin' married! Don't act like you don't see that wedding ring he's wearing," she barked, jabbing her finger in the woman's face.

"Ashton, chill." Damacio spoke calmly, reaching for her hand.

"Get the fuck off me!" she snapped, flinging her arm, smacking Damacio in the face. He knew how hot tempered his wife could be, so he kept his cool, not wanting things to go nuclear.

"Baby, there's nothing going on. We were just talking."

"Oh, so when you're out here, this is how you interact with females? Letting these thirsty chicks feel up on you. Cool. Well, let me go follow your lead and you tell me, how you feel about this shit," Ashton popped. She exited the VIP area in search of the perfect prey, which would be easy pickins, with the slinky jumpsuit she was wearing. But Damacio wasn't having it. Once Ashton ignited the tit for tat game, he knew things might turn deadly rather quickly.

"Don't start this bullshit!" Damacio rumbled, rushing after his wife, with his security detail right behind him. "I know you hear me talkin' to you!" He grabbed her from behind, causing Ashton to stop in her tracks.

"Get your hands off of me!" Ashton swung on Damacio again but this time he was already on the defense and able to block her shot. He was tempted to toss her over his shoulder, on some caveman type shit but deaded the idea. Instead, he pinned Ashton's arms behind her back, pushing her towards a hallway entrance where a bathroom was.

"Clear everyone out of that bathroom!" he ordered one of his security to do. A few seconds later, a couple of men came out, mumbling curse words, wondering what the hell was going on.

"Let me go!" Ashton continued yelling but Damacio ignored her bawling and kept a firm grip on her arms.

"It's all clear, boss," the security detail informed him.

"Both of you, stay posted outside this door and don't let anyone in until I'm done." Damacio shoved Ashton inside the bathroom, slamming the door. "Why must you do dumb shit like this?" he shouted, pounding his fist, against the wall.

"This is my fault? You're the one in a club with some chick who isn't your wife! Are you fuckin' her?" Ashton fussed, with an accusatory glare. "Are you!" Her voice got louder and louder. She began beating Damacio in the chest with her fists, taking his silence as an admission of guilt.

"No, I'm not fuckin' her or no other woman," he finally said. "I only want you," Damacio held her chin up and said. The calmness of his voice, in contrast to her aggression seemed to settle Ashton.

"But she was so close to you and I saw her hand on your leg."

"I wasn't paying her any attention but I'm sorry you had to see that." Damacio placed his hand on the nape of Ashton's neck. "I miss my wife. I miss holding you, kissing you," he said brushing his thumb across her lips. "Feeling inside of you."

"I miss you too." Ashton leaned in and kissed Damacio. Each kiss became more intense and passionate as their lust took over. Within seconds, Damacio had his hand on the back closure of Ashton's jumpsuit, unzipping it. He cupped her breast, then placed her hardened nipple in his mouth as Ashton moaned with pleasure. Before long, she was slipping out her clothes giving Damacio easy access. Ashton unbuttoned Damacio's pants, wrapping her long leg around his waist as he gripped her ass. "Aaah, mmmm, I missed this dick so much," Ashton cried out when Damacio entered inside of her.

With each powerful thrust, Ashton's pussy got wetter and wetter. She was insatiable, unable to get enough of the warmth she felt, as Damacio's thick dick seemed to be going deeper, completely consuming her insides. She bit down on his neck, to keep herself from screaming out in pleasure and pain.

"You belong to me, you know that right," Damacio uttered in Ashton's ears between strokes.

"Yes...always. I love you more than anything," she whimpered, as a warm sensation ripped through her body causing her to shake uncontrollably. She buried her face in his neck, taking in his masculine scent. Ashton had no idea she was capable of feeling such sexual gratification, until the first time she had sex with Damacio. It wasn't until him, she'd experienced an orgasm and he made sure she had one every time they made love.

While Ashton was getting dicked down in the bathroom,

Vannette was on the other side of the club dealing with her own dilemma. The reason she went missing after they first entered the venue, was because she caught a glimpse of Brianna grinding against Clayton on the dancefloor. Her initial reaction was to break down crying. Seeing the man she was in love with, dancing with a woman she once considered a good friend, was painful. Vannette had hoped Brianna and Clayton's relationship was simply a sexual fling, that would die down quickly. To see them out, enjoying themselves like a couple, made her want to vomit. Instead of becoming an emotional wreck, Vannette took a step back and asked herself, what would Ashton tell her to do in this situation. *Fuck! Let me see if I can pull this off,* she thought to herself, making a beeline for the bar.

Vannette was a very pretty girl, who didn't naturally tap into her sex appeal. Her style was more understated and for the most part, it worked for her, that was until Brianna became her competition. If it had been any other man, Vannette would've stepped aside and moved on to someone else. But she had it bad for Clayton. For her, it couldn't get any better than him. She knew in order to compete with Brianna, she would have to step out of her comfort zone.

"Make me an Absolut Bitch please," Vannette told the bartender. Ashton had turned her on to the tasty, yet potent drink. It was the liquid courage she needed to try and get a rise out of Clayton. By her third shot, Vannette was beginning to feel less inhibited. She pulled out her phone and used the camera to look at herself, as she reapplied her lip gloss. She then fluffed out her hair and unbuttoned her blouse low enough, that her ample breasts were on full display. Luckily, she had on a cute lace bra, so it appeared to be a part of her ensemble. With those few adjustments, the men began circling like vultures. She kept declining their offers to buy her a drink and or dance, until one man had enough appeal to do some damage.

"I'm Jeremiah and you are?"

"Vannette." She gave the handsome man a flirtatious smile.

"Vannette, can I buy you a drink?"

"I guess I can have one more," she happily accepted. "I want you to do something else too. Dance with me."

"Sure." After buying Vannette another drink, he took her hand and off they went.

Vannette led Jeremiah to the section of the dancefloor where Brianna was still grinding up against Clayton. She made sure to appear oblivious to their presence, all while finding the perfect location where the spotlight appeared to be shining directly on them. The Absolut Bitch, which consisted of Absolut Vodka, Bailey's Irish Cream, Kahlua and Tuaca, had completely snuck up on her. She began to feel like the world around her was changing into a magical place. Her dance partner had plenty of babe magnet qualities, so it was easy for Vannette to morph into a full fledge sex kitten and Jeremiah was eating it up.

"Damn, you sexy," he said, holding Vannette close. She was playing a flirty game of pulling away and then allowing Jeremiah to draw her back in. Their playful yet seductive moves, soon had people taking notice, including Clayton and Brianna. Initially, neither realized the sultry beauty they both seemed to be enamored with, was someone they knew but that quickly changed.

"Is that Vannette?" Brianna questioned first, slowing down her grinding.

"I believe so." Clayton stated. Brianna could tell by the coldness in his tone and the way he was eyeing the duo down, Clayton wasn't pleased.

"I'm thirsty. I'm sure you are too. Let's go back to the table and have a drink," Brianna suggested, becoming unsettled with the amount of attention Clayton was paying Vannette.

"You go ahead. I'll join you shortly," he said, headed straight towards Vannette.

Brianna was fuming at the fact Clayton left her standing all alone, so he could go confront her rival. She wanted to curse him out but knew it would defeat her purpose, of trying to win him over. Clayton was a tough nut to crack and playing the jealous girlfriend, wouldn't help her cause. Instead, Brianna lurked in the background, dissecting their interaction.

Clayton stood, observing the pair for a moment, before speaking up. "Vannette, it's good seeing you here. How are you?"

"Oh hey, Clayton," she waved casually, while continuing to dance with Jeremiah. At this point, Vannette had reached an epic buzz and was genuinely enthralled in her interaction with Jeremiah. However, her unintentional diss worked in her favor. Clayton felt a tinge of jealously at seeing the woman he frequently treated as an afterthought, pay him dust because she was enjoying another man's company. His overinflated ego wasn't amused.

"Can I speak with you for a moment?" Clayton managed to ask through clenched teeth.

"In a minute," Vannette brushed him off and said, moving closer to Jeremiah, whose hands were placed at the arch of her back.

Clayton stormed off, refusing to lose his cool. "Let's go." He told Brianna when he got back to the table.

"But we haven't even been here an hour."

"And...you're welcome to stay but I'm leaving. Are you coming or not?"

"Let me finish my drink," Brianna said, taking the last few sips. She blamed Vannette for Clayton's sudden mood change. Their evening was going perfect until she showed up on the scene. *Either that bitch has perfect timing or she planned this shit,* Brianna thought to herself as she grabbed her purse and followed Clayton out the door.

Chapter Eleven

Can't Run From Love

"I was hoping you would join me downstairs for a drink," Allen said to his wife, when he entered their bedroom.

"I can't. I'm actually heading out." Karmen had her purse in hand and was looking for her keys.

"Where are you going at this time of night?"

"I'm meeting Gayle for drinks. With everything that has been going on with Kasir and Ashton, I haven't had a chance to see her. She invited me out and I accepted."

"I see. Where are you all going?" Allen questioned.

"Just to The Remington Bar. I'm not sure when I'll be back, so you don't have to wait up."

"For the last few weeks, you've been doing everything possible, to avoid having meaningful dialogue with me about the state of our marriage. We're living in the same house, sleeping in the same bed but it feels like we're strangers. This has to end, Karmen."

"There's nothing left for us to discuss. I already told you this marriage is over." Karmen stared her husband directly in his eyes and affirmed. "If Ashton was in a better place emotionally, I would've already filed for divorce. I'm done with you."

"You'll never be done with me. Yes, I fucked up again. Getting involved with Crystal was a terrible mistake but that's behind me. When she asked to see me one last time, I should've said no. There's no excuse for my poor judgement but a misstep I had with some woman, isn't worth destroying our marriage over."

"Misstep...that's what they're calling affairs now? I've learned something new today," Karmen mocked. "Now excuse me, I don't want to keep Gayle waiting."

"You can't do this!" Allen stepped forward, blocking the entryway of the door. "I'm not going to let you tear this family apart."

"No! You tore this family apart when you started fucking that woman! That same woman found her way into our son's bed too but I'm sure you already aware of that!" Karmen spewed.

Allen swallowed hard. He wasn't expecting his

wife to hit him with facts he couldn't dispute. "I found out the day Kasir was shot. I wasn't aware they were seeing each other and that's the truth."

"Oh, I believe you. The great and mighty Allen Collins would never stand for his mistress sleeping with his son," she retorted sarcastically. "How dare she!" Karmen cut her eyes. "The only silver lining in this travesty, is I was able to get rid that poison you brought into our life before she destroyed our son, the way she destroyed our marriage. Now move out of my way."

Allen didn't recognize the woman standing in front of him. She looked like his wife but she sure as hell didn't sound like her. There wasn't a trace, of the woman he planned to spend the rest of his life with and he found it alarming. Fear wasn't a trait Allen ever embraced but coming to the realization his marriage might be over had him petrified.

"I'm not giving up on us," Allen stated, stepping aside. But the way Karmen brushed past him without a second glance, made him wonder if he even stood a fighting chance to win back his wife.

"Yo, this the second time this month that niggas money short. What's the problem?" Caesar questioned Jeff, tossing the duffel bag full cash on the floor.

"Man, TJ said business been slower than usual. We

ain't the only party in town no more. Yo' connect Alejo, told you we would have everything on lock. It was like that for a minute but shit done changed," Jeff popped.

"He's right," Darius nodded. That nigga Flint who handles shit way over in Austin, mentioned there's been an influx of product hitting the streets his way too."

"Why you ain't mentioned this to me?" Caesar demanded to know.

"I figured eventually we would have some competition but nothing that would stop our money," Darius said.

"The money ain't stopped," Jeff interjected. "TJ just bringing in a little less than before but we still stackin' that paper."

"Nah, this shit ain't acceptable. Right now, we ain't feelin' the pinch. But if it stay like this, three or four months from now, our pockets will start hurtin'." Caesar shook his head.

"So what we gon' do?" Jeff questioned.

"Find out who floodin' the streets wit' this extra product and eliminate them. There can only be one king." Caesar contended.

"Boss, I'm down for whatever but I don't think this the right time to take any drug wars to the streets. It's already hot out here. Any more violence, might bring unwanted attention to our organization. We don't need that," Darius argued, trying to be the voice of reason.

"I always like a little gunplay," Jeff laughed, "But, Darius right. We been keeping a low profile. I think that's why we've been able to make so many moves and go undetected. As soon as niggas start dying and the bloodshed begin, is when yo' crew is labeled a menace to society and they shut you down. We makin' way too much money to let that bullshit happen."

Caesar wasn't trying to hear all that but he knew his boys were right. This wasn't the time to start fuckin' up by making dumb mistakes. He had to move wisely. There was way too much money on the line.

"A'ight. No violence for now but still find out who's behind this shit. When it's time to make our move, I need to know who we're targeting," Caesar huffed.

"Affirmative. We on it," Darius agreed.

"Good. We'll get up tomorrow," Caesar said, getting up from the chair.

"You not going out wit' us?" Jeff asked, sounding surprised.

"Nah, not tonight. I'm expecting somebody."

"Don't tell me you back wit' Brianna," Darius shook his head.

"Nope. That shit dead. Ain't no resuscitating that."

"Then who?" Darius and Jeff both questioned.

"Niggas, mind yo' business," Caesar cracked, as they all laughed. "Let's go. I want you gone before she gets here," he said walking them to the door.

"We leaving man, damn! You ain't gotta throw us out, like you would a bitch wit' bad pussy," Jeff joked, pretending to fall over as Caesar opened the door.

"Hi. I didn't realize you had company. I can come

back." Karmen smiled graciously, when she saw the three men standing in front of her, before she even had a chance to knock.

"No! They're leaving. Please, come in," Caesar said, reaching out to take Karmen's hand.

"Talk to you later." Darius and Jeff said to Caesar as Karmen walked past them.

"Man, that woman look mad familiar." Jeff squinted up his face trying to remember where he knew her from. "She don't look familiar to you?" he asked Darius, as they were getting in the car.

"Nah, she don't," Darius lied and said. He knew exactly who she was. Even after all this time, he remembered Caesar becoming instantly enamored with the sophisticated beauty, when she walked into The St. Regis Hotel. He also recalled Caesar telling him she was a married woman. He warned his childhood friend, to leave her alone and he was pissed, Caesar ignored his advice. *This won't end well,* Darius thought driving off.

"You had me worried. I was starting to think you wasn't coming," Caesar said, wrapping his arms around Karmen before kissing her.

"I'm sorry. I got held up at home for a little bit."

"Is everything straight? Nothing else has happened with Ashton or your sons has it?" Caesar questioned, leading Karmen over to the couch, so they could sit down.

"No, nothing like that," she assured him.

Caesar continued holding Karmen's hand and held

it up. "I see you still wearing your wedding ring. What happened to you leaving him?"

"I am, that hasn't changed."

"Does your husband know that?"

"Yes. I made it clear to Allen it's over between us. That's the reason I was late getting here. He wanted to discuss the state of our marriage and I told him the truth," Karmen clarified.

"Then why are you still wearing your ring and living in the same house with him, instead of living here with me?"

"Caesar, I want to be here with you. I really do. I hate sneaking around and lying to my children but Ashton is going through a difficult time right now. Being home with her mother and father, is giving her the stability she currently needs."

"What about Damacio? I would think she'd want to me with her husband." Karmen slipped her hand from underneath's Caesar and stood up. He had a feeling he knew why she was pulling away. "You don't have to hold back. You can trust me," he insisted.

"I do trust you but..." Karmen stopped mid-sentence.

"But what?"

"It's complicated."

"I can handle complicated." Caesar smiled, trying to put Karmen at ease.

"Damacio's father is a man by the name of Alejo Hernandez. Alejo used to do business with my husband

and it ended badly. He doesn't approve of his son being married to my daughter and it's vice versa with Allen. But Alejo is the one who had Ashton kidnapped."

"What? That's fucked up." Caesar had yet to tell Karmen the line of business he was in, or that Alejo was his supplier. Karmen had no idea, he was aware of the dynamics between all the players involved.

"Exactly. I've known Alejo for many years and never did I believe he would do something so heinous to my daughter. Of course Ashton finding that out, has put a strain on her marriage."

"Which is understandable."

"I was prepared to tell her earlier today about my plans to divorce her father but she's not ready. She went through something traumatic and I don't want to bring more chaos to her life right now. But I'm optimistic. For the first time since the kidnapping, Ashton went out with her friends tonight."

"That's a good sign. I think your daughter will be fine. She's strong like her mother."

"You're sweet," Karmen said, walking back over to where Caesar was sitting. "I don't want you to think I'm playing games with you."

"You betta not be." Caesar stared at Karmen and stated.

"I'm not. I'm married to Allen in name only. You're the one I want to start this new chapter of my life with. All I'm asking is you be patient and give me a little more time."

"I do lack patience but I'll learn to have it for you." Caesar lifted Karmen's hand and kissed it. "You're everything I want in a woman and more. But don't make me wait too long."

"I won't."

Unwilling to wait any longer, for what he wanted most at that moment, Caesar pulled the tie waistline on Karmen's sage green knotted floral print dress. With no effort, it slipped open revealing a matching silk nude bra and panty set. The smoothness of her skin appeared to glisten, against the contrast of the silk. Caesar ran his hand up and down the curve of her waist, admiring every inch of her body.

"You're perfect." He seemed to be looking inside her soul. Caesar was so anxious but instead of rushing, he decided to maintain his composure. He lifted Karmen from the couch and carried her upstairs to his bedroom. He wanted to take his time and make love to her like no other, so she would want to fall asleep in his arms every night, for the rest of her life.

Chapter Twelve

Lose Control

Damacio turned over in bed expecting to feel Ashton by his side. After a few more seconds, when he realized her warm body wasn't next to his, he opened his eyes. He glanced over at the clock and saw it was a little after 1pm. When he looked around the bedroom, he noticed Ashton's clothes draped on the chaise lounge. He figured she was downstairs in the kitchen, getting something to eat. But when Damacio got out of bed and was on his way downstairs, he heard some noise coming from the master bath. He headed towards the bathroom, hoping Ashton was in the shower and he could join her. Although they had sex at the club last night, then came home and made love off and on for hours, Damacio still hadn't had enough of his wife. He was hoping they could make love again, with the hot water drenching their body.

When he entered the bathroom, Ashton was naked, standing near one of the sinks, with the water running. At first, Damacio thought she was washing her face but he could see the gray marble counters contrast sharply with the white powder spread across the top. Ashton flipped her long hair over her shoulder, bent down and began snorting a line of coke she'd already cut with a razor. Damacio instantly became enraged.

"This is why you wanted to stay at your parent's house...so you can put this fuckin' poison up your nose?!" he roared, gripping Ashton by the back of her hair. Damacio held her head firmly and shoved it towards the mirror. "Look at you!" he continued to yell before pressing her face in the coke on the marble counter.

Ashton began coughing profusely as the coke got in her throat and nose. "I can't breathe," she gasped. "Pleaaaaase Damacio, let me go!" Ashton pleaded.

"You disgust me!" he fumed, releasing Ashton from his grip. She began splashing water on her face and spitting the coke out of her mouth.

"Why would you do this to me?" she cried, reaching for a towel to wipe her face.

"Do you really have to ask such a dumb fuckin'

question!" Damacio scoffed. "Just look at yo'self in the mirror."

"You're overreacting for no reason. You knew I dabbled in drugs before we got married. I never lied to you!" Ashton protested loudly.

"You said you would stop! You think I wanna be married to an addict? You're so fuckin' weak. I can barely stand to look at you."

Seeing the disgust on Damacio's face made Ashton want to breakdown and cry. She hated to disappoint her husband but instead of confessing how defeated she felt at this moment, she chose to lash out.

"You think I'm so fuckin' flawed! That you're better than me. I'm fed up with trying to live up to your impossible standards. I'll never be good enough for you. Isn't that why your father had me drugged, thrown in a back of a van and held against my will because I wasn't worthy of his perfect son. Fuck you and him!" Ashton wailed, grabbing the vase off the counter and throwing it at Damacio's head. He ducked, just in time as the glass shattered against the wall.

"Typical spoiled brat behavior. Your parents created a monster indulging you so fuckin' much but I'm done entertaining this shit. Get the fuck out...now!" Damacio demanded.

"You're kicking me out of my own home? Our brand new mansion!" Ashton stood dumbfounded.

"You said you didn't feel safe here, remember. You wanted to be at your family's estate, where you felt secure with mommy and daddy. Well get yo' shit and go be with them. You can do all the coke you like. Try not to OD on it." Damacio scolded.

"I hate you! I hate you...I hate you...I hate you!" Ashton screamed repeatedly before rushing out the bathroom to get her stuff. She slipped on her jumpsuit, not even bothering to put on her shoes, storming out the house, wanting to get far away from Damacio before he saw her face drenched in tears.

Vannette woke up on her living room floor with a migraine headache, wearing the same clothes from last night. She couldn't even remember how she got home. Instead of trying to figure it out, she took some aspirin and headed straight to the shower. The hot steam seemed to relieve the throbbing that made her feel like her head was about to explode.

"I can't believe I drunk so much," Vannette sighed, allowing the water to saturate her hair. Flashbacks of last night began to trickle into her memory. She remembered becoming consumed with jealousy seeing Brianna and Clayton together, then trying to dish some payback. "I guess it didn't work," she huffed, turning off the water and getting out the shower.

Vannette was about to go lay back down, when she heard the doorbell. "I bet that's Ashton," she said, putting on her bathrobe before going to open the door.

"Good afternoon."

"Clayton." She stood speechless for a moment. He liked never came to her apartment, maybe once, twice at the most. *Maybe my scheming to get Clayton's attention worked after all*, Vannette thought to herself. "What are you doing here?"

"I came to see you. Do you have company?"

"No, why would you ask me that?"

"Last night you appeared to be busy. I wasn't sure if that busyness followed you home." Clayton wasn't concealing his distaste for what he saw last night. "Are you going to let me in or what?"

"Sure, come in." Vannette stepped to the side, allowing Clayton to pass by.

"So, who was he?" Clayton asked when they got to the living room.

"Huh?"

"The guy who was all over you on the dancefloor."

"Oh him. He's just a friend." Vannette kept it vague, enjoying seeing this jealous side of Clayton.

"You let all of your friends feel up on you like that?"

"Just the ones I like," she giggled.

"You think this is funny?"

"It was a joke, Clayton."

"Is he the reason you didn't answer my call yesterday?"

"No, I didn't have my phone with me. I called you

back but you didn't answer."

"By that time it was too late."

"Too late for what?" Vannette asked.

"I wanted you to accompany me to a dinner I was having with a business associate. When you didn't answer, I asked someone else."

"Really and who did you invite instead?" Vannette knew the answer to her question but wanted to see if Clayton would tell her the truth.

"Brianna," he divulged without hesitation.

"I'm sure she was more than happy to be your date. I know Brianna prefers to be paid for her services but I'm guessing she gave you the prime package deal for free," Vannette hissed sarcastically.

"I can see Brianna being well compensated for her services. She's very good at what she does but you're right, she hasn't felt the need to charge me. I guess because we're mutually pleasuring each other."

"I can see that. Kinda how Jeremiah and I mutually pleasured each other last night." Clayton knew how to jab the knife but instead of letting him twist it in her heart like she had in the past, Vannette decided to jab it right back.

"You fucked him?" Clayton stepped forward. The smug look on his face vanished. He was used to crushing egos, not having someone crush his.

"What do you think?" Vannette replied with a haughty smirk, turning her back on Clayton.

"You think you can fuck somebody else," Clayton

scoffed, grabbing Vannette's arm. "That pussy belongs to me."

Vannette felt herself completely aroused. Her pussy had never gotten wetter, than it was at that moment. "If it's yours than show me," she mouthed, taunting him.

Clayton took the bait. He ripped open her bathrobe, exposing her naked body that was still slightly damp from her shower. He threw her down on the couch and spread her legs, putting his tongue deep inside her sugar walls.

"Clayton!" Vannette screamed out, unable to contain herself. Each lick had her body shivering. His mouth and tongue glided through her lips with precision and excellence.

"You taste so good." Clayton paused for a second, staring at Vannette intently and said. He was blowing her mind without even trying. She began kissing him passionately, while tearing off his clothes. She needed to feel his rock hard dick inside her, like a dope fiend desperate for a fix.

"Please fuck me," Vannette begged, wrapping her legs around his back.

"Damn!" Clayton moaned, sliding every inch inside her. "You so fuckin' wet." Vannette almost felt like virgin pussy to him. This was the first time they ever had sex without using a condom. Each stroke was like swimming in a warm body of water. If it wasn't his pussy before, Clayton was going to make sure it was now.

"I love you Clayton," Vannette whispered, wishing he would stay inside of her forever.

"Then why you give my pussy away?" he beseeched, gripping Vannette's neck while dicking her down.

"I didn't. I swear. This pussy belongs to you. It always has," she cried, pressing her nails in Clayton's back.

Clayton's dick got even harder after Vannette's admission. His strokes became more intense. Seeing the love, passion and desire in her eyes made him want to pound her insides out, feeling that he couldn't get deep enough. It wasn't until they both climaxed simultaneously, did Clayton finally get the complete satisfaction he longed for.

Chapter Thirteen

Severing Ties

Kasir had finally been discharged from the hospital a few weeks earlier. He was told to take it easy and he did but after having around the clock care at his home, he was feeling like himself again and relieved to be back at work.

"Looking good behind your desk," Clayton winked, coming into his brother's office. "You've finished your first week back, on a high note but I wouldn't expect anything less from my big brother."

"It really does feel good to be back in the office,

behind my desk. Thank goodness for youth. If you can survive a perilous surgery, your recovery rate is much quicker," Kasir nodded, leaning back in his chair.

"True and luckily you're in excellent physical shape. I mean you hit the gym almost as much as I do. But I'm just thankful to have my brother back. I can't lie, you had me scared for a minute," Clayton conceded.

"What? Mister, I'm not afraid of anything, Clayton Gabriel Collins," Kasir chuckled.

"Damn, you had to state my full government name to make your point? Listen, I can admit, I have feelings and emotions like everyone else."

"I already knew that. Remember, I'm the big brother. I was right there, while you were growing up. You like to make people think you're heartless but I know the real you."

"Next topic," Clayton cracked, ready to move on. "It's Friday, thought I have an early dinner. Why don't you join me. I'm buying."

"How about give me an hour and I'll meet you. I need to make a quick stop first," Kasir said, clearing off his desk before getting ready to leave.

"Sounds good. I'll text you what restaurant to meet me at."

"Cool."

"But seriously Kasir, it really is good to have you back. Sometimes you don't fully comprehend how much you want a person in your life, until you risk losing them."

"I love you too, bro." Kasir hugged Clayton, knowing that's what he was trying to say but had a difficult time saying the words. "I'll see you shortly for dinner and don't forget, it's on you. Make sure you pick one of those ridiculously expensive restaurants you love so much," Kasir laughed.

"You already know my style," Clayton said, following his brother out the door.

Ashton and Vannette were having a late lunch but there wasn't much eating going on, at least for Ashton. She wasn't herself and her friend couldn't help but take notice.

"This is different," Vannette shrugged, playing with her grilled chicken salad.

"I'm not following you. What does that mean?" Ashton questioned, sipping her wine.

"Normally, you're extra bubbly and I'm the one in a funk but today it's the opposite. You haven't touched your food, although you love the sea scallops and truffle fries here. What gives?"

"Honestly, Damacio is furious with me."

"I thought you all were back together? You left with him when we were at the club a couple weeks ago. What could've happened between then and now?"

"I haven't seen him since then, I just didn't tell you.

I thought we would've made up by now but he's being so fuckin' stubborn," Ashton griped.

"What is he mad about?" Vannette was curious to know what would keep Damacio away from Ashton, since they seemed to be madly in love.

"It's so stupid. When he woke up the next day, he walked in the bathroom and caught me snorting a lil' coke. He freaked out," she said, shaking her head.

"Damacio didn't know you dabbled in drugs?"

"Duh, of course he knows. I never hid it from him. I even tried to get Damacio to do some with me but he spazzed out, like I was trying to get him to rob a bank with me or something."

"What's his hang up? It's not like you're some crackhead addict on a corner."

"Exactly but Damacio wants a wife who's as pure as the driven snow. That ain't me and he knew this before he put a ring on it. It's infuriating because I miss my husband so much but he has to dominate everything," Ashton complained.

"I know how much you love him. Maybe you should give up the coke to make peace," Vannette suggested.

"First it's coke, then it'll be the clothes I wear. After that, it'll be something else. I'm not ready to turn my life over to Damacio but I can't let him go either," Ashton sighed. "Enough of this depressing talk about my husband. What has your glow on ten? Don't think I didn't notice. Is it a new guy in your life? You have that,

I'm getting freshly fucked on a regular glow." They both giggled.

"I must admit, I do but it's not a new guy. It's a tried and true one."

Ashton had a bewildered look on her face, like she didn't have the slightest clue who Vannette was talking about. "Well, are you going to tell me or what!" she remarked, taking the new glass of wine, the waitress brought her.

"Who do you think....Clayton!" Vannette announced. Thinking the answer should've been obvious.

"My brother is responsible for this good mood and glow you have...wow! He's normally the cause of you moping around feeling depressed."

"I know but I tried one of your tricks and it worked."

"Which trick?"

"You know, use a cute guy as prop to make the intended target jealous," Vannette stated proudly.

"If you do it right, that trick is practically bullet proof. I can't believe you pulled that on my brother? Where was I when this was going down?"

"It was that night we went to the club and you left with Damacio."

"Are you serious! I would've given anything to see that go down."

"Yeah, at first I didn't think it worked. He actually came to the club with Brianna."

"He's still fuckin' with that skank?" Ashton frowned.

"Yep, or at least he was that night. I was devastated when I saw them together. I literally wanted to run out the club in tears but I stopped and asked myself, what would my girl Ashton do. I got myself super tipsy, loosened up and found the perfect guy. Granted, Clayton didn't lose it at the club."

"Of course not. He's much too arrogant for that," Ashton laughed.

"Yep but he showed up at my apartment the next day, interrogating me. He showed a jealous streak, I've never witnessed before."

"Me neither and I've known him all my life."

"Bringing out those emotions, was like striking gold because we had the best sex ever and he's been putting it down on a regular ever since."

"Bitch, kudos to you!" Ashton beamed, lifting up her wine and Vannette did the same. "Well fuckin' played!" she cheered, clicking their glasses together.

When Kasir pulled up to the apartment complex, he sat in his car, debating if he should go in or not. His mind told him to drive off but a combination of his heart and curiosity made him get out. He kept practicing what he would say when the door opened but when he knocked, all his preparation faded into oblivion.

"Hi, can I help you?" the petite brunette asked.

Kasir did a doubletake to make sure he knocked on the right door. It was the correct apartment number but he was completely unfamiliar with the chipper white girl who answered.

"Yes, my name is Kasir. I'm here to see Crystal."

"Crystal? There's no Crystal here."

"Really...maybe I did knock on the wrong apartment door," Kasir wondered out loud, second guessing himself.

"I did just move in a few weeks ago," the woman said, trying to be helpful. The handsome man, dressed in an expensive suite, standing at her door, appeared harmless, so she was more than willing to assist him, if she could. "Hold on one moment. Some mail has been coming here. Let me see who's name is on it. I'll be right back."

"I appreciate that...thank you." Kasir's friendly smile, made the tenant feel comfortable enough to leave the front door wide open. He could clearly see from the layout, this had indeed been the apartment, he visited Crystal at several times.

"Yep, Crystal was the previous tenant," the woman grinned brightly. "There are several pieces of mail addressed to her. Are you a relative or friend? I can give you her mail if you like. She didn't leave a forwarding address," she said, handing the small pile of envelopes to Kasir.

"You can keep it. I won't be seeing Crystal again but thank you for your help." Kasir smiled graciously.

"No problem. Feel free to come back if you like," she called out, wishing she had invited the handsome gentleman inside.

Kasir headed back to his car, wishing he had listened to what his mind was telling him and kept it moving. At least then, he could've continued to suppress the speculating as to why Crystal had disappeared out his life. But now that he allowed himself to seek out answers, Kasir was more curious than ever to figure out how this woman he cared for deeply and shared a connection with, had now vanished.

What is going on with you Crystal? Your phone numbers are disconnected. The apartment you only recently moved into, you leave in a hurry with no forwarding address and you haven't tried to contact me once. Could your life be in danger, he thought to himself, driving off. Kasir couldn't let this go. He was determined to find out what happened to Crystal and why she walked out his life.

Clayton was handing his car keys to the valet when he noticed someone he was well acquainted with, across the street. Kasir had just called him saying he would be late, so Clayton had some time on his hand. He rushed to catch the woman, before he lost track of her.

"You're a hard woman to get in touch with. I

thought you left town," Clayton said, blocking Crystal's path.

"I knew I should've stayed away from this side of town," she cut her eyes at him. "This is where all the self-righteous, rich pricks gather."

"Then why are you here?"

"Remi needed me to pick up something for her because she couldn't get off work in time. If I knew I'd run into you, I would've told her to figure it out."

"Aren't you being exceedingly cocky for some-one who barely qualifies for a minimum wage job and should be in desperate need of money at this point, which of course I'm able to supply. I know my brother hasn't been seeing you, nor my father, so where is all this bravado coming from? Or is this fake confidence for my benefit?"

"I don't need your money anymore, Clayton. I've figured out another way to make it just fine."

"I find that hard to believe. You are good at what you do but you're not that bright to secure the bag on your own. You require lots of guidance, unless you now have a pimp."

"The last pimp I had was you," Crystal scoffed. "You left such a bad taste in my mouth. I decided never again. Now if you'll excuse me, I have someplace to be," she spat.

"You're not going anywhere until you tell me what happened. The last time I saw you, my father kicked you out the hospital and you were desperate to find out what happened to Kasir. Even going so far, as threatening to expose our arrangement, if I didn't keep you informed of my brother's progress."

"Which obviously didn't work since I never heard a word from you!" Crystal bickered.

"I guess that's why you had your friend, sneaking around the hospital, asking questions."

"You knew about that?" she inquired.

"Haven't you learned by now that I know everything."

"Not everything," Crystal teased.

"I suggest you stop feeling yourself, or have you forgotten that with one phone call, I can have your ass thrown back in prison," Clayton reminded her.

"How long do you plan to hold that over my head?" Crystal wanted to know.

"I haven't decided yet but for now I want you to answer my question. I know how you felt about my brother, so why did you up and disappear?"

"Let me put it this way, the Collins family is the gift that keeps on giving," Crystal stated with disdain.

"Wait. I find it hard to believe my father paid you off, after finding out he'd been sharing his mistress with his oldest son." Clayton raised an eyebrow in disbelief.

"I never said it was your father," Crystal countered with defiance.

Clayton felt a lump in his throat. "My mother paid you off?"

"Neither you or Allen Collins, has anything on

that woman. That lady is freezer cold." Crystal shook her head, remembering the family matriarch's threats. "Part of our agreement was for me to move immediately, change my numbers and never reach out to Kasir again. But on the bright side, your mother said I was more than welcome to keep screwing her husband. Of course Allen was done with me anyway and I only wanted to be with your brother. I didn't get Kasir but I received a cute piece of change to get ghost."

"This wasn't the outcome I was expecting."

"Surprisingly, I agree with you and I'm relieved this is over. Your family is ruthless. I don't understand how someone as kind as Kasir, can be related to any of you."

"You're right, our family is ruthless. Including Kasir. Don't let my brother's calm disposition fool you. But I our business relationship is officially over," Clayton agreed. "I have no intentions of going against my mother's wishes."

"Why am I not shocked. Your mother can be very persuasive."

"Yes, she can."

"Does this mean, no more threats of having me thrown back in prison, if I don't let you play puppeteer with my life?" Crystal asked.

"Like I stated, it's over. You take care of yourself. Enjoy your freedom but a word of advice. Don't cross my mother, so make sure you stay away from Kasir. It's one and done with her," Clayton warned.

Crystal wasn't sure what to make of Clayton's parting words but she wasn't in the mood to overanalyze it. For the past year, every aspect of her life had been intertwined with a member of the Collins family. Now that the cord had been severed, there's was no turning back. Crystal's previous life died, when Karmen Collins cut the check.

Chapter Fourteen

Listen To Your Heart

"You have a visitor," one of the staff members who worked at Damacio's club said, nodding his head towards the entrance. "I'll go in the back, so you can have some privacy."

Damacio turned towards the entrance and his wife came strutting through the door, looking fresh faced and flawless. The flattering flared fit, mid blue distressed jeans was paired with a nude chevron mesh, long sleeve thong bodysuit, strappy heels and a nude clutch. Ashton was wearing minimal makeup, mascara, hint of blush, to accentuate her high cheekbones and her favorite Fenty gloss bomb. Her long hair was draped over her right shoulder, which showcased the diamond studs Damacio had gotten her as a gift, when they first started dating.

"Since you wouldn't take my calls, I had no choice but to come here in the middle of the afternoon, to see my husband. Ignoring me, isn't going to fix our marriage, Damacio."

"Ashton, you wasted your time coming here. I don't have anything to say to you."

"I'm not a child, Damacio! You can't put me on timeout until you believe I've learned my lesson, before letting me out my room. I'm your wife. We're supposed to be equals."

"You want to be my equal, then act like it. Because currently, your behavior is that of a spoiled, self-centered child."

"I'll admit, I have some selfish ways but I'm willing to work on it. I love you and I want to come home," Ashton said, placing her purse on top of the barstool, next to where Damacio was sitting.

"You think it's that easy. Just state what Ashton wants and everyone will fall in line to grant your request. That might work with everyone else in your life but not with me. It's time for you to grow up."

"I get it! You think I can be immature...fine! But I can't change overnight. It's a process and I want to go through the process together, instead of apart."

"Where was all this togetherness when I was begging you to come home?" Damacio responded.

"You know the hell I went through when I was kidnapped!"

"No I don't because you shut me out and wouldn't tell me what happened while you were gone! You did nothing but push me away!" he shouted angrily.

"You left me no choice. You refused to believe your father was responsible for keeping us apart. You still won't accept it," Ashton snapped.

"For argument sake, let's say my father had you abducted. He didn't keep us apart once you came back. You made the choice to stay at your parent's house, instead coming home with me, your husband. Now you decide you're ready to be my wife again and I'm supposed to let you come back with open arms. It doesn't work like that, Ashton."

"I never stopped being your wife. I was dealing with a lot of stuff and I still am but..." Ashton put her head down, trying to push out the images of that man attacking her. "The point is, I love you and I know you love me too. I want to make our marriage work. I'll do whatever it takes."

"Even give up the drugs?" Damacio grilled.

"I'll give up the coke...okay," Ashton agreed, becoming flustered.

"All drugs. The pills...everything, Ashton," he insisted.

"Why are you doing this? You're trying to turn me

into some saint. That's not who you fell in love with. You were attracted to me. A girl who breaks the rules not conform to them."

"You're right. When I saw you that night in Miami at the club, you were practically making love to yourself, while dancing in your own world. You were sexy, beautiful with an aura of mystique." Damacio brushed the side of Ashton's face. "I decided right then, I had to have you."

"And you do have me. I'm standing right here and I'm asking you to let me come home, so we can be together again. Listen to your heart. Don't you miss me?"

Ashton gazed lovingly at her husband. She had this sweetness, a subtle innocence that couldn't be erased even with her party girl lifestyle. It was the reason Damacio continued to be captivated with his wife, although he hated she loved putting that poison in her body.

"I always miss you, even when you're standing right here next to me." Damacio kissed his wife passionately before abruptly stopping. "No more drugs, Ashton."

"Okay," she nodded. Willing to say anything, so her husband would stop talking and get back to kissing.

"And I want you to go to rehab," he added.

"Excuse me!" she exclaimed. "Did you say rehab?" Ashton stepped away from Damacio becoming defensive.

"Yes. I can't take your word you're going to quit on your own. You have a drug problem and I don't want you coming back home, until you agree to get help."

"You have got to be kidding me. I'm not sticking a needle in my arm, shooting up heroin. Or smoking from a crackpipe. How dare you stand there being so fuckin' sanctimonious. Your father is the head of one of the largest drug cartels. I'm sure that same drug money made it possible for you to have all these fuckin' clubs you own!" Ashton admonished.

"There you go. Flipping the switch. This has nothing to do with me and how I conduct my business. This is about you and your drug habit and why you rather put that crap up your nose, instead of dealing with your problems."

"Stop psychoanalyzing me. I'm not some pet project you need to fix!" Ashton mocked.

"Stay on topic," Damacio advised coldly. "Will you go to rehab?"

"I told you I would stop using drugs. My word should be enough for you." Ashton began fidgeting with her bracelet. She felt like Damacio was pushing her into a corner and it made her skittish.

"Your word isn't enough. Either agree to rehab or else..."

"Or else what?" Ashton interrupted Damacio. "It sounds like you're giving me an ultimatum."

"I call it a choice. Either drugs or our marriage. I won't be married to a woman who lacks self-control to the point, they can't stop abusing drugs."

"I'm not having this conversation with you right now. The last thing I need, is unnecessary stress. I have to go!" Ashton grabbed her purse off the barstool and ran out.

Ashton was struggling to find her phone when she saw Vannette was calling. Initially, she was going to send it to voicemail but there were already three missed calls from her friend, so she answered.

"Hello."

"How can he do this to me! I don't understand why he has to be so cruel!" Vannette bawled.

"Calm down and tell me what happened." Ashton found her key, got comfortable in the car and listened to Vannette pour her heart out. She knew this had to be about her brother because he was the only person, who could get her friend this riled up.

"I decided to surprise Clayton and stop by his place to bring him an early birthday present."

First mistake, Ashton said to herself. *Never surprise a man like my brother. There's no telling what you might discover, showing up unannounced.*

"Okay, what happened?" Ashton questioned when Vannette stopped talking and burst into tears again. She was stuttering and sounded like she was hyperventilating. "Vannette, take a deep breath. You have to relax. Breathe."

Ashton could hear Vannette taking deep, repeated breaths from the gut. Her cries of immense sorrow were diminishing. Once the sobbing ceased, Vannette continued telling her story.

"As I was driving up, I saw Brianna's car parked in the driveway. She got out and when Clayton opened the front door, his tongue was down her throat. You should've seen them, standing there just kissing. It was disgusting!" Vannette hollered.

"I'm sorry you had to see that."

"We've been spending so much time together. I thought he was done with Brianna and wanted to be with me."

"If you and Clayton are supposed to be in an exclusive relationship, then you need to confront him. He can't just cheat on you!" Ashton fumed.

"Technically he isn't cheating," Vannette pined. "He never said we were exclusive. Like a dumbass, I assumed. Why doesn't he love me," she said sadly. "Maybe he doesn't think I'm pretty enough."

"Omigosh! Are you crazy! You're freakin' gorgeous. You look like the woman on that show my mother loves so much. Fuck! What's the name of it." Ashton was snapping her fingers, trying to remember. "The Haves and the Have Nots!" she blurted. "You look like the chick Candance. She has that cute President guy, begging her to be First Lady."

"That's television, this is real life."

"I know it's television. The point I'm making is, you're beautiful. Don't let my moronic, conceited brother, make you doubt yourself. Your better than that, Vannette."

"But why her and not me."

"If it wasn't Brianna then it would be some other chick. It's not you, it's him. Clayton isn't ready to be in a committed relationship and he might never be. I hate you torture yourself like this. Where are you?"

"Parked up the street from Clayton's house."

"Vannette, you can't be serious. This isn't healthy. Listen, meet me at the mall. We'll do some shopping, go out to eat and hit a lounge later on. We can listen to some music, dance, drink. Fun shit that doesn't require you to think about Clayton. I need to let off some steam myself. Damacio is driving me crazy too," Ashton complained. "What do you say?"

"I say that's a great idea and I'm so lucky to have you as a friend. Thanks, Ashton. I'm feeling better already," Vannette was smiling through the phone.

"Perfect! I'll see you soon." When she got off the phone with Vannette, Ashton noticed Damacio watching, as she sat in her car. She was tempted to run back to her husband and confide in him what happened while she was kidnapped. Then beg him to be patient with her. That eventually she would completely stop using drugs but not make her go to rehab because she was capable of stopping on her own. Instead of facing her fears, Ashton pulled out the parking lot and drove off.

Chapter Fifteen

Don't Leave Me

"Kasir, it's wonderful to see you," Karmen beamed hugging her son tightly. "Since you've gotten better, you're impossible to track down."

"I'm sorry. I've thrown myself into work. I had a lot of catching up to do but I should never be too busy for my mom."

"No worries. You're here now. You should stay for dinner. Bernice just finished cooking. I know how much you love her food." Karmen latched her arm through Kasir's, walking him towards the dining room.

"That would be nice. Is Ashton here?"

"No. Your sister is with Vannette. She said, they'll be out late, so don't wait up."

"Sounds like Ashton. Before I eat, is dad around? I needed to speak with him about something."

"Yes. He's in his office. You go speak with your father and I'll have Bernice make you a plate."

"Thanks, mom," Kasir smiled, giving his mother a kiss on the cheek before going to see his father. "You got a minute?" he lightly knocked on the office door, that was slightly ajar.

"I always have time for my eldest son. Come on in," Allen waved his arm. "Sit down and relax. Can I pour you a drink?" he offered.

"I'm good."

"Are you staying for dinner? I'm sure your mother already put in her request."

"She did and of course I said yes."

"I'm sure. I don't think anyone likes telling your mother no."

"Very true but luckily I am hungry and Miss Bernice is one hell of a cook but that's not the reason I stopped by. I came to see you."

"Really...what's going on?"

"You haven't been back to the office since you went out of town for business last week."

"Yes, I've been working from home. I wanted to spend some time with Ashton and your mother."

"Is everything okay between you and mom?" Kasir inquired.

"We're working through some problems. When you've been married as long as me and your mother has, you occasionally experience bumps in the road."

"Does those bumps have anything to do with your infidelity?" Kasir decided to delve a little deeper.

"Excuse me!" Allen shut his laptop, caught off guard by his son's accusation. "Where is this line of questioning coming from?"

"Months ago, Clayton mentioned mother told him you were having an affair."

"And only now, you're telling me this?" Allen frowned up his face.

"He told me in confidence. I didn't want to betray my brother's trust but since you brought up, the two of you are having problems, I had to ask."

"I made a mistake." Allen hated to admit. "But I believe your mother will forgive me," he stated, becoming resentful, he had to explain himself. "I'm sure your mother isn't the reason you came to see me." He had no desire to discuss his marriage with Kasir.

"No it isn't. I wanted to speak with you about Crystal."

Allen shifted in his chair. "What about her?" he kept his head down, pretending to be preoccupied with something he was reading.

"She's the woman, who was with me when I got shot. I'm sure you must've spoken with her."

"Yes, briefly. She came to the hospital."

"What did Crystal say?"

"I don't recall. As I stated, it was brief," Allen shrugged.

"Dad, try to remember," Kasir pressed.

"Why is this so important to you?"

"Because I care a great deal about this woman and I'm concerned she's in some sort of trouble."

"Why would you think that?" Allen questioned.

"Because she's vanished. A few weeks ago, I stopped by her apartment and she moved."

"Son, people do move."

"I know but she moved to this apartment complex recently. Why would she up and leave, unless she was running from something," Kasir theorized. "Her phone number is even disconnected. Crystal wouldn't run off without getting in touch with me first, unless she wasn't able to. Dad, you have a lot of connections. Please help me find her," Kasir pleaded.

"Kasir, you don't think you're overreacting? I mean how much do you really know about this woman. Or, maybe she was involved in some illicit activities, which required her to disappear in a hurry."

"You might be right but I need to know for sure. Dad, will you help me? You can use that same guy, who dug up all the dirt on one of our competitors, that was trying to undermine a huge deal we were closing on."

"I know who you're talking about. But..."

"Please dad," Kasir implored, knowing nothing

positive came after the word but, when it came to his father.

"Fine. I can't promise you anything but I'll have Vincent look into it. Give me all the details you can about this Crystal woman and I'll pass it along to him."

"Dad, thank you. This means a lot to me. I really care about her. I just want to know she's okay."

"I understand, son. I'll do what I can." Both men stood up. Kasir walked around his father's desk to shake his hand. The handshake turned into Kasir giving his father a hug to show his gratitude.

"The table has been set. It's time to eat dinner," Karmen entered the room and announced.

"We were just finishing things up in here," Kasir said, patting his father on the shoulder. "Dad is helping me out with something. I was giving him a hug to show my appreciation."

"That's wonderful, son," Karmen smiled sweetly.

"Yes it is. Now let's eat!" Kasir clapped his hands.

"You go ahead, Kasir. Let me speak to your father for a second. We'll be in there to join you shortly."

"Cool. Play nice," Kasir joked, leaving out.

Karmen went to make sure Kasir was gone, before closing the office door. "I overheard part of your conversation with our son. He asked you to help him find Crystal. I'm assuming you agreed to help him, not to arouse suspicion. But you know when Kasir becomes fixated on something, he won't let up."

"I'll handle it. I know how to deal with Kasir. But

what I'd like to know, is why are you discussing our personal issues with Clayton?"

"If you mean the divorce, I felt he had a right to know."

"First of all, there won't be a divorce and second, I'm talking about the infidelity. When Kasir asked me about Crystal, for a second I thought he was aware of my dealings with her. Luckily, I'm cautious and play things close to the chest. I could've easily slipped up."

"Dealings...you mean affair," Karmen said, flippantly. "In regards to Clayton, a few months ago, he sensed something was bothering me. I do regret sharing the information with our son but I was feeling vulnerable at the time and he was there to listen. I didn't think he would confront you about it."

"He didn't, however Clayton told Kasir. You better hope neither one of them tell Ashton."

"I better hope? Oh please Allen, this is all on you."

"We both know how sensitive Ashton is. She's finally getting back to normal after her ordeal. Finding out her father cheated, would more than likely cause a major setback."

"I'm aware of this, Allen. Ashton has always put you on a pedestal. Blindly idolizing you. I have no desire to be the one to tarnish this perfect image she's created. It's the main reason I haven't filed for divorce yet. My only concern is what's in the best interest of our children."

"There's no denying, you're an exceptional mother. The wellbeing of our children has always been your first priority."

"And it continues to be. That's why I'm hellbent on making sure, Kasir never discovers the truth about your relationship with Crystal. Learning he and his father were sharing the same woman, would cause catastrophic consequences. Believe me, I don't want our son to hate you."

"I have no intentions of letting that happen," Allen assured his wife.

"Then you better make sure Kasir never finds Crystal. It's in this family's best interest, she stays missing. Now excuse me, I'm going to join our son for dinner."

Allen wanted to erase any evidence of his affair with Crystal. Out of sight, out of mind. If she was no longer an issue, he believed he could save his marriage. But with Kasir's newfound mission, of locating his lady love, Crystal would remain a constant reminder of his infidelity to his wife. He began to consider all of his options and one in particular, seemed to be the most appealing. Allen decided he needed to get rid of Crystal, permanently.

"Girl, you always come through. I've been having a blast!" Vannette gleamed, hugging Ashton.

"It's still early. The night is only gonna get better," Ashton smiled widely, filling her glass with more champagne. "Oh shit! What did I just tell you! This my fuckin' song!" Ashton jumped up, when the beat dropped on the Cardi B song Money. She started rapping along like she was on stage performing.

Look
My bitches all bad, my niggas all real
I ride on this dick in some big tall heels
Big fat checks, big large bills
Front, I'll flip like ten cartwheels
Cold ass bitch, I give Ross chills
Ten different looks and my looks all kill
I kiss him in the mouth, I feel all grills
He eat in the car, that's Meals On Wheels,
Woo!

"Get it, Ashton!" Vannette hyped her friend up while she grinded to the music.

"We might need to hit the strip club next, so I can do some tricks on the pole," Ashton laughed.

"Tonight, I'm down for whatever," Vannette chimed in, loving how lively Ashton was. She admired how her friend was able to shake off the bad and have a good time. Vannette was trying to learn to do the same but it wasn't easy. Although she was having a fantastic time with Ashton, Clayton stayed heavy on her mind.

"Vannette, I'll be right back. I'ma go chat it up with my ex, right quick."

"Take your time. I have plenty of bubbly to keep me company."

"Cool!" Ashton blew her a kiss and hurried off.

From the short distance, Vannette saw Ashton sit down in a corner booth with two guys. *That looks like her ex-boyfriend, Grayson. I wonder if he's just in town visiting or he moved back to Houston,* Vannette was thinking to herself until becoming distracted by a text message from Clayton. She stopped clocking what her friend was doing and began communicating with Clayton via text.

"You're still gorgeous as ever," Grayson commented, kissing Ashton when she sat down next to him.

"Thanks, you're still sexy as fuck too," she teased.

"I didn't think you were gonna come over and speak. I've been calling and texting you but no response."

Ashton put her left hand up and wiggled her fingers. "It's beautiful right."

"You got married!" Grayson pulled Ashton's hand close to his face. "I can't believe it," he shook his head in disbelief. "When I used to talk about marriage, you would always scream you were way too young to even consider it."

"Well, things change."

"I see." Grayson glanced back down at the massive diamond ring on Ashton's finger. "I used tell your father,

I would be the one who would marry you. How is Mr. Collins doing?"

"My dad is great. I'm sure he would've been thrilled if I married you, or somebody like you."

"I take it, he doesn't care for your new husband?"

"That's putting it nicely but enough about that, what are you doing here? I thought you had taken a position as a finance manager at some big time firm in New York City?"

"I did but they're looking for someone to head up their new office here in Houston. Of course, I'm their first choice," Grayson boasted.

"Good for you."

"How's school coming?" he asked.

"I decided to take a semester off, being a new wife and all. Have some fun," Ashton giggled, pulling out a small vile of cocaine with a telescopic spoon. "This booth is perfect. I don't have to sneak off to the bathroom. It's nice and private over here. You want some?" she offered to share some of her coke.

"Nah, I'll pass. I have an early meeting tomorrow. I try not to mess with that stuff unless I have a long weekend off."

"I get it. Luckily, I sleep late," Ashton said, taking a hit. "Remember that one guy you knew...he used to have the best coke. This stuff is decent. I mean it gets the job done," she smiled.

"Does it still get you open?" Grayson asked, stroking Ashton's hair. "We used to have some of the best sex after doing a few lines."

"Get the fuck up. Now!"

The reverberating voice sent a chill down Ashton's spine. Her body jerked forward, knocking her vile of coke on the table. "Damacio, what are you doing here?" she asked nervously.

The white powder instantly caught Damacio's eyes. "You whoring yourself out for coke now!" he barked.

"Man, don't speak to her like that," Grayson shouted, about to stand up.

"Grayson please, it's okay. This is my husband."

"I don't care. He has no right to speak to you like that."

Please stay out of this!" Ashton pleaded.

"I advise you to listen to my wife because this won't end well for you," Damacio warned.

Grayson noticed two formidable looking men standing off to the side, eyeballing him. Their gaze was steady and resolute. He then glanced down at Ashton who slightly shook her head, letting him know to take heed to her husband's warning. Grayson wisely took her advice.

"Damacio it's not what you think. I..I..I..." Ashton couldn't even get her words out. He reached down and yanked her up by the arm.

Grayson leaped forward and his friend who was sitting with him, stood up to hold him back. He saw what the goons standing off to the side was reaching for.

"You fuckin' disrespect me. In this place, snorting coke, letting this man touch you, put his hand in your hair...acting like a fuckin' whore! You disgust me!" Damacio spit on the floor.

"It's not like that I swear!" Ashton protested.

"You stand here and you lie to me! I saw you with my own fuckin' eyes!" Damacio was gripping her so tightly, you would've thought he was going to break Ashton's arms.

"Damacio, let her go!" Caesar came up from behind and said. He placed his hand on Damacio's shoulder. "You need to calm down," he urged. "It's the wrong place for this." Caesar had been at the lounge, having drinks with some new buyers when he noticed the commotion across from his booth. When he realized it was Damacio and Ashton, he knew he had to intervene.

Damacio's breathing was rapid. His rage had him not thinking sensibly. Caesar showed up at the right time, before he went over the edge. He was a passionate man but also extremely logical and he knew to take Caesar's advice.

"I'm done here." Damacio stated calmly, releasing Ashton.

"Yes, baby let's just go home." Ashton reached out to take his hand but her husband pushed it away.

"I don't think you understand. I'm done here and that includes me being done with you." Damacio's words cut deep.

"Baby, you don't mean that. We're everything to each other." Ashton stroked Damacio's face, wanting to remind him, of how deep their love for each other was.

Damacio held Ashton's hand firmly, looking her directly in the eyes. "I don't want you anymore. You're not worth the trouble," he said before turning to Grayson. "You can have this junky. She's all yours." Damacio scoffed, letting Ashton's hand go and walking off.

"Damacio wait! Don't leave me!" she cried, chasing after him.

"Ashton, let him go." Caesar stopped her.

"He can't leave like this! We love each other."

"And you will work it out but not right now. You need to let him calm down. Running after Damacio while he's this upset, will only make it worse."

"What have I done," she sobbed, laying her head on Caesar's chest.

"It'll be okay. Damacio will come around." He patted Ashton on her back. Caesar felt bad for her. He knew she was a very troubled young lady. "Take her home," he told Vannette, who was standing behind them. She was still in shock after seeing the drama go down between Ashton and Damacio.

"Of course. Come on Ashton, let's go." Vannette held her friend's hand. Ashton was still visibly distraught. She wanted the love of her life back but was scared it might be too late.

Chapter Sixteen

I'm The Only One For You

"Good morning," Brianna smiled, when Clayton came in the kitchen. "I didn't think you were going to ever wake up."

"I guess I should blame you. You had me put in quite a workout last night," Clayton remarked, pouring himself a glass of orange juice. "Something smells good in here."

"Yeah, I figured when you woke up, you'd be hungry. I'm almost done and I'll fix you a plate."

"I never figured you as the cooking type."

"I have a lot of skills you haven't had a chance to tap into yet," Brianna teased.

"As long as you maintain your skills in the bed, we're good," Clayton remarked.

"I hope I'm not just a great fuck to you. I know I'm not sweet like Vannette but I want to be more than just a great lay."

"Where is this coming from, Brianna?"

"I can tell you like her. You tried to downplay it but you were upset seeing her at the club with another man."

"If I saw you with another man, I would be upset. I'm just territorial like that. Ask my brother and sister. Growing up, I never liked them to touch my shit and I still don't."

"I see. So, we're not special to you."

"Brianna, you are special to me." Clayton stood behind her, wrapping his arms around her waist, kissing her neck. "And so is Vannette. I enjoy both of you for different reasons. Do you have a problem with that?"

"Of course not," Brianna lied.

"Good. Because I can be the only territorial one in a relationship. Now let's eat and then go back to bed. Morning sex is my favorite," Clayton said, biting down on her neck.

"Whatever you want, baby. I'm here to please you."

Brianna knew all the right words to say. Her relationship with Caesar prepared her for Clayton. She learned from her previous mistakes and planned to be much more strategic with cementing a permanent position in Clayton's life.

"This is really nice. I wish we could stay longer," Karmen said, looking out the vast window in the penthouse suite.

"I don't see why we can't. I'm game if you are." Caesar didn't want their weekend to end.

"I'm sure you are but I have to get home. Coming to Dallas for a getaway was a great idea but we have to get back to Houston."

"I get it but I'm selfish. I don't want to let you go," Caesar said pulling Karmen down on the bed.

"It felt good being out, not feeling like we had to sneak around."

"Yeah, I got to show you off. When we walked into that restaurant, all those men were staring at you. Wishing they could switch places wit' me," Caesar grinned.

"Stop playing," Karmen laughed.

"I ain't playin'. Dead ass serious. But you know you're beautiful. I can't wait until I don't have to share you anymore and you're all mine."

"You're not sharing me now. I haven't been intimate with Allen since we started seeing each other." Karmen wanted Caesar to know.

"I believe you but I need more. I wanna come home to you. Treat you like the queen you are."

"It'll happen."

"It better but listen." Caesar sat up in the bed, getting serious. "I've been wanting to talk to you about something."

"This isn't about my divorce? You told me you would give me more time."

"No, it's not that."

"Then what?"

"I know how protective you are about your kids and I don't want to cross the line but I care about you. I'm lying," Caesar paused. "It's more than care. I'm in love with you, Karmen."

Her eyes widened. Karmen wasn't expecting Caesar to say those words to her. "I'm not sure how to respond."

"I don't want you to feel like you have to say it back to me. You may not be in love with me yet but it'll happen," Caesar said without hesitation.

"It already has. And I'm saying it because I mean it. It feels kinda strange. When I first fell in love, I was so young and naïve. Now, I'm this grown woman and I'm falling in love all over again. It actually feels better the second time around," Karmen beamed.

"You have no idea how good it feels to hear you say

that," Caesar admitted, kissing Karmen passionately. He wanted to make love to her again, right then but what he had to say couldn't wait.

"Why did you stop? I know I said we needed to get back to Houston but we have a little time left," she said leaning back in to kiss Caesar.

"First, let me tell you this."

"Okay, say it so we can get back to having some fun."

"How's Ashton doing?"

"She's fine. Why are you asking me about Ashton?"

"Is she back living with Damacio?"

"Not yet. What is with all these questions about my daughter?"

"Did Ashton tell you about a huge blowup she had with him a couple weeks ago at a lounge?" Caesar questioned, trying to determine what Karmen knew.

"No! They were fighting?" Karmen stood up. "Did it become physical?" she asked angrily.

"No but it was heated. Damacio was extremely upset. He saw his wife with another man and..."

"That has to be a mistake!" Karmen exclaimed, cutting Caesar off. "Ashton's madly in love with Damacio. She would never cheat on him."

"Karmen, I need you to calm down and listen."

"Alright, I'm listening."

"Please sit down." Caesar was reluctant to tell Karmen this but he felt she had the right to know. "I believe Ashton has a drug problem."

"Why would say something like that?" Karmen's face filled with grief.

"One of the reasons Damacio was so upset, was because she was doing cocaine and it wasn't the first time."

"Dear God, this can't be true." Karmen put her head down and kept shaking it. "How long has this been going on?"

"I'm not sure but at least since that shooting at Damacio's club," Caesar said, remembering the incident Brianna told him about.

"Omigosh, that was months ago. Do you think she's an addict?" Karmen felt nauseated.

"I don't know if your daughter's an addict but I believe she needs help."

"What kind of mother am I, that I didn't even know my daughter was using drugs." Karmen's eyes filled with tears.

"You're a great mother." Caesar held Karmen in his arms. "I don't have any kids but I can only imagine how hard it must be to keep track of everything they do. I remember being Ashton's age and trust me, I was in so much shit. Till this day, I'm stunned my mother survived it. Don't beat yo'self up."

"What am I supposed to do?"

"Be there for her. Get Ashton the help she needs before it's too late."

Karmen took Caesar's advice to heart. She would do whatever necessary to save her daughter. Ashton needed her mom now, more than ever and Karmen had no intentions of failing her.

"I can't believe you still haven't spoken to Damacio," Vannette said, while they were getting their pedicure. "I thought he would've come around by now."

"Me too but then again, I've never seen him that angry at me before. He won't take any of my calls or respond to my texts. I even stopped by the house a few times but he wasn't there. I'm tempted to give up." Ashton contemplated.

"Are you serious? But you love Damacio."

"I do but I can't make him stop being mad at me. I was even tempted to go out to dinner with Grayson the other night."

"He's still in town...he hasn't gone back to New York?"

"Nope. I think he's job is going to have him here for a while."

"Grayson is a cutie and everything but you were never crazy about him like you are about Damacio."

"True but at least Grayson accepts me for who I am. He doesn't make me feel like such a loser," Ashton sulked.

"Damacio's older than you and very protective."

"Yeah but I'm tired of fighting with him. When we

first met everything was so intense and exciting. Now things are different."

"Ashton, of course I'm on your side but when you got serious with Damacio, I remember you telling me you stopped doing drugs. You said being in love gave you the ultimate high and you didn't need it anymore."

"Yeah, I remember but things change," Ashton said sadly.

"What could've happened to make things change so drastically, that you started back using so much?"

Ashton hadn't even realized how frequently she'd been using coke, until this very moment when Vannette asked that question. Instead of facing her demons, she chose to suppress them. But the only way for Ashton to do that was by using more drugs.

"Vannette, isn't that your friend?" Ashton questioned, glad to have an excuse to get off the subject of her drug use.

"Oh my fuckin' goodness, it's Brianna," Vannette seethed.

"Gosh, not her ass," Ashton mumbled, now regretting she said anything. "I knew she looked familiar but I didn't realize that was the girl messing with my brother."

"Damn sure is. Here she comes. I hope the nail tech doesn't sit her next to me," Vannette spat.

"Hey pretty ladies!" Brianna smiled being extra bubbly. "I had no idea you all went to this nail salon too," she said sitting in the chair next to Vannette. "Ashton, I love that tie front shirt you have on. It's really cute."

"Thanks." Ashton kept her response extra brief.

"I called you last week. I was inviting you for lunch. I left you a voicemail, did you get it?" Brianna asked Vannette, who refused to look in her direction.

"Yeah, I got it."

"Is there a reason you didn't call me back?"

"What do you think?" Vannette snapped, turning to face Brianna.

"I thought we agreed we wouldn't let my relationship with Clayton, come between our friendship."

"Your relationship?" Vannette frowned. "A man having sex with you at his convenience doesn't qualify as a relationship."

"Although Clayton and I do have great sex, we also do other things together," Brianna countered.

"Like what?"

"A few weeks ago, I was his date for a fancy dinner he had with a business associate," Brianna bragged.

"Only because I missed his phone call. He wanted me to be his date. You were his second choice."

"Ouch. This is getting good," Ashton said under her breath, leaning back in the chair, enjoying the front row view. The nail technicians were pretending not to listen but they were all in the mix too.

"You liar!" Brianna retorted.

"You wish I was lying! How 'bout I show you the text messages," Vannette hollered, taking out her phone.

"So what! That was weeks ago. You might've been

his first choice then but I'm Clayton's first choice now!" Brianna taunted. "Who do you think he woke up next to this morning," she sneered.

"You're such a skank! Isn't that what you called her, Ashton?" Vannette turned to her friend and said.

"I call everybody that." Ashton kept her reply very nonchalant, like it was no big deal. She wasn't in the mood to get in the middle of their catty exchange.

"You can say whatever you want, Vannette. As long as Clayton likes it, I'm good. And by the way I had him saying my name this morning, he likes it a lot," Brianna shamelessly boasted.

"Shut your mouth!" Vannette screamed reaching over to grab Brianna's neck but got ahold of her necklace instead.

"You bitch! You broke my necklace! Do you know how much this cost!" Brianna roared.

"Vannette, chill!" Ashton barked, realizing it was time to play mediator. They were on the verge of tussling with each other in the nail salon. Ashton got out her chair and stood between the women, who were ready to go to blows. "Both of you stop!"

"I can't believe I ever considered you a friend!" Vannette fumed.

"Oh please...stop whining!" Brianna huffed.

"Vannette, put your shoes on and let's go," Ashton said taking out her wallet to pay the nail techs. "Here, we'll come back another day."

"She should be the one to leave, not us," Vannette

complained, as Ashton practically dragged her out the salon.

"Girl, one more minute in there, they would've called the police. Them Chinese folks, not gonna let you all tear up their shit. I wouldn't be surprised if they about to toss Brianna's ass out," Ashton fussed, getting in the car.

"I know I shouldn't of showed out but that chick just irks me." Vannette was still pissed.

"I get it but you can't let her get under your skin. Either leave my brother alone, or you're gonna have to deal with the fact, he's fuckin' with both of you."

Vannette couldn't figure out if she was angry that Clayton was seeing another woman, or was it because that woman was Brianna. At this point it didn't matter, she simply wanted her former friend out of the picture. Vannette felt she was the better woman for him and she had to make Clayton see it too.

Chapter Seventeen

Keep The Family Close

Listening to Vannette complain about Brianna had worn Ashton out. After dropping her friend off, she was relieved to be home and looked forward to taking a hot shower. She was headed straight upstairs, until seeing her mother in the den watching television.

"Oh hey, mom! I'm wasn't expecting for you to be home until tomorrow," Ashton said, giving her mom a hug. "How was your spa retreat?" she asked, delighted to see she was home.

"It was very relaxing but I'm happy to be back.

I missed you," Karmen said, not letting up on their embrace.

"I missed you too but you can let me go now," Ashton giggled.

"I'm sorry. I feel like we haven't been spending enough time together. Why don't you sit down and watch television with me."

"I would but I really want to go upstairs and take a shower. Probably pop a couple of aspirins too. Vannette and Brianna gave me a serious headache," Ashton grumbled.

"Who's Brianna?" Karmen wasn't familiar with her name.

"She used to be friends with Vannette but now she's dating Clayton. Which of course, Vannette is furious about. Her and Brianna were about to kill each other at the nail salon. I didn't even finish getting my pedicure done." Ashton threw up her hands, becoming aggravated all over again.

"Dramatic much."

"You have no idea. I don't get why either one of them would fight over Clayton. He's never going to settle down. He's way too in love with himself."

"I think your brother will end up surprising you. I see him meeting the right woman and getting married in a few years."

"Well, God bless the woman who marries him because she is setting herself up, for never ending stress. I wonder if Clayton even knows the drama he's causing between Vannette and Brianna. It doesn't matter. It's not like he would care. He's not thinking about them or marriage."

"Speaking of being marriage, when are you going home to your husband?"

"Are you trying to rush me out the house? I thought you enjoyed having me back home, living here with you and dad," Ashton said coyly.

"You know I love having you here." She rubbed her daughter's arm affectionately. "But I know this is only supposed to be temporary and I'm sure Damacio wants his wife home with him."

"Damacio understands we need time apart."

"Really?"

"Yes...do you remember Grayson?"

"Of course. Your father still mentions him from time to time. He took a job in New York...right?"

"Yeah but he's back. I ran into him a couple weeks ago. We're going out to dinner tonight."

"Do you think that's a good idea?" Karmen asked. "Going out to dinner with your ex-boyfriend. I doubt your husband would approve."

Ashton glanced around the room nervously. "I didn't want to say anything but Damacio and I are having problems in our marriage. I'm having a difficult time dealing with what his father did to me and Damacio has a problem with how I'm coping with it."

"How are you coping, Ashton...is it with this?" Karmen held up a small plastic bag containing cocaine.

"You were in my room...going through my stuff!" Ashton tried to grab the bag from her mother's hand but she moved it out the way. "Why would you do that?"

"The more important question is why would you have this in the first place? Isn't your drug use the real reason you're having problems with Damacio?"

"Have you spoken to him?" Ashton wanted to know.

"No, I haven't but I heard about the altercation the two of you had, at some lounge a couple weeks ago."

"Who told you about that?"

"It doesn't matter. How long have you been using cocaine, Ashton?"

Ashton rolled her eyes, not wanting to answer the question but she knew her mother wasn't going to let up. "I've been using it off and on for a couple years now, mostly socially. It's really not a big deal."

Karmen had to exercise restraint. She remembered what Caesar told her and having a screaming match with her daughter, wouldn't be beneficial. She wanted to reach Ashton, not push her away.

"Recently, how often have you been using cocaine? I ask because I find it hard to believe, you would have a bag hidden in your room, for occasional use." Karmen was doing her best to get to the truth without speaking to Ashton in an accusatory tone. She could see her daughter processing the question and considering how to answer.

"Truthfully," Ashton hesitated and her eyes watered up. "Every day. Sometimes twice a day." Then she burst out crying. "It's the only thing that numbs the pain."

Karmen just held her daughter, allowing her to cry for a few minutes without saying a word. She was harboring an enormous amount of pain and this was the first step to Ashton freeing herself.

"Come on, let's sit down," Karmen suggested, once Ashton's sobbing decreased and she regained her composure. "I want to thank you for telling me the truth. You could've easily lied and denied but you didn't."

"I guess because I was ready to get it out in the open. I tried to forget about what happened but that's impossible," Ashton said, looking down. "I can't pretend any longer. When I was kidnapped, one of the men almost raped me. Saying it out loud makes it real."

"Ashton, I'm so sorry. I knew something terrible happened but I was trying to wait and let you tell me when you were ready. I should've pushed harder."

"No, it would've made it worse. I wasn't ready to deal and if you never confronted me about the coke, I probably would've stayed in denial."

"Are you ready to talk about what happened now?"

"Not really but I know I need to. It's probably the only way I can escape this mental nightmare, I'm consumed with on a daily basis. I am grateful there wasn't any actual penetration but my goodness, he came so fuckin' close." Ashton got choked up again.

"Take your time." Karmen didn't want her daughter to feel pressured. She had been traumatized enough.

"His pants were down. He ripped off my underwear and pried my legs open. He was about to force himself inside me and would've, if Chi hadn't walked in and pulled that monster off me. I can still smell his scent." Extreme rage consumed Ashton, reflecting on that moment.

"How horrific." Karmen wished death upon the savage who brought her daughter such agony but right now, it wasn't about him. "Who is Chi?"

"He was one of the kidnappers. He's the guy who told me it was Alejo that hired him. It was strange because Chi was really nice...I mean for a kidnapper," Ashton shrugged. "He always made sure I had good food. It's like he knew exactly what I liked. I never felt scared around him. I know that sounds weird but it's true. But I guess my feelings were right because he saved my life. If it wasn't for Chi, I would've been raped and beaten."

"I'm grateful for that too but none of this should've happened to you in the first place. Alejo will pay dearly for what he's done. I promise you Ashton." Karmen could almost taste the venom.

"Trust me, I want that too. I feel like Alejo will always be an issue between me and Damacio. I'm not sure if....Omigosh!" Ashton screamed out all of a sudden.

"What's wrong?!" her mother felt frantic.

"Turn up the volume on the television!" Ashton yelled.

Karmen grabbed the remote and both of their hearts dropped. Breaking news flashed across the television screen.

Local business mogul, Allen Collins has been rushed to the hospital, after being shot while exiting his office building, located in Downtown Houston...

Mother and daughter didn't wait to hear anything else. They grabbed their belongs and sprinted out the house, praying for the best.

Kasir and Clayton were already at the hospital when they saw their mother and Ashton running in panic stricken.

"Mom!" Clayton called out, putting up his hand.

"What happened to daddy...is he okay!" Ashton wailed, thinking the worst. She reached her brothers first but their mother was close behind.

"Please don't tell me your father's dead." Karmen's hand, covered her mouth. After keeping a vigil by Kasir's bedside, she never wanted to step foot inside another hospital again. Yet here she was, this time for her estranged husband.

"Both of you can relax," Clayton assured them.

"Yes, dad is going to be fine." Kasir nodded. "The bullet only grazed his right shoulder but dad's driver wasn't so lucky."

"Jackson's dead?" Karmen gasped.

"No. Jackson was off. You didn't know that?" Clayton asked his mother.

"I went out of town for a couple days. I only got back today, so I didn't realize Jackson wasn't working," she explained to her son.

"This driver was filling in for Jackson. From what I understand, he saved dad's life," Kasir informed them.

"Oh goodness, that poor man. He's family will be devastated. We have to make sure they're taken care of," Karmen insisted.

"I'm already on it," Clayton said, not wanting his mother to worry.

"That's horrible about the driver but thank God daddy's okay. I couldn't take losing our father," Ashton exhaled, holding on to Clayton's arm. "We have to keep the family close. We're all we have."

"Neither could I," Karmen acknowledged.

The four of them gathered close and held each other. Irrespective of their differences, they knew it was imperative to stick together. Allen Collins was the patriarch of their family and they would rally around him no matter what.

Chapter Eighteen

Can't Let Go

"Baby, it's so good to see you." Caesar held and kissed Karmen before she was even inside the house. "I haven't seen you in over a week and barely talked to you."

"I'm not sure if you heard but Allen was shot," Karmen said, standing in the foyer as Caesar closed the door.

"No, I didn't hear anything about it. I haven't had much time to watch the news. Is he okay?"

"Yes. A bullet grazed his shoulder but other than that he's fine. Unfortunately, his driver didn't make it."

Karmen put her head down. It saddened her an innocent man loss his life.

"Come on, let's go sit down. Can I get you something to drink. You know I make sure to keep your favorite wine in stock," Caesar grinned.

"A glass of wine sounds nice."

"That's terrible about the driver but I'm glad your husband is fine," Caesar said, going into the kitchen to pour Karmen a glass of wine.

"Thank you for saying that about Allen and for the wine. I need it. It's been a very stressful week." Karmen sat down and finished her drink rather quickly. She was tempted to ask for another glass but opted against it.

"I can tell you're tense but it's understandable."

"It's not only Allen but also Ashton. When I got home that day, I went to her room and looked around. I found her hidden stash of cocaine."

"Damn, I hate to hear that. So this drug situation is serious," Caesar shook his head.

"Yes, it is. Very serious. She's been using daily. Ashton said she's been dabbling in it for the last couple years but it escalated after the kidnapping."

"That makes a lot sense. Going through something like that would fuck anybody up but especially young girl like Ashton."

"But that's not the worst part. One of the men who abducted her also tried to rape her. My poor child was assaulted and terrorized."

Caesar could see Karmen was on the verge of

breaking down and went to comfort her. "I hate Ashton had to go through that and for you to feel the pain too. It ain't right."

"It's not and I don't care what I have to do, Alejo will suffer dearly, for doing this to my child. I'm almost positive it was him who tried to kill Allen but with their business dealings, I get things like that can happen. But for Alejo to drag my daughter into this madness is unforgivable." Karmen exploded.

"Baby, try to calm down. You're absolutely right and Alejo should be dealt with," Caesar agreed.

"I wish I could also find the sonofabitch who tried to rape my daughter. But Ashton doesn't know his name. Only the other kidnapper, Chi who saved her life. I want to kill him and thank him at the same time. How ironic is that," Karmen huffed, baffled by the entire ordeal.

"I know how much you love Ashton and it's impossible for you not to stress but focus on your daughter and don't worry about those men. They'll be handled. Muthafuckas like that can't escape karma."

"I pray you're right for Ashton's sake and mine. But you're absolutely correct, I have to focus on Ashton and my family."

Caesar scooted back away from Karmen. It was something about the way she said my family, that didn't sit well with him. "Is there something more, you tryna tall me?" he questioned.

"Caesar, you've been amazing for me. I never thought it was possible for me to be intimate with another man, let alone fall in love. But I did fall in love with you and you'll always have a special place in my heart." Karmen lovingly stroked the side of Caesar's face.

"Why does this sound like the end?"

"Because it is. I have to go back to my family which includes Allen. Finding out Ashton has a cocaine addiction, then Allen getting shot...it's all too much. If I leave my husband, our family would fall apart. I believe her drug addiction would spiral even furher out of control and poor Kasir. If he ever found out the woman he cared about is the same woman his father had an affair with, it would destroy him and their relationship. Then Clayton." Karmen had to shake her head, thinking of her youngest son. "I believe his dislike for his father and his need to protect me, is the reason he can't emotionally commit to one woman."

"Then it should be obvious how toxic your husband is to you and your family. Why would you stay?"

"Because if I stay, I can keep our family together but if I leave, all of their lives will go to shambles including mine. I know they're technically grown but if my kids aren't good then neither am I."

"Karmen, I told you I would be patient. That hasn't changed. I want you here with me but I respect your loyalty and the love you have for your family. But that isn't a reason for things to end between us."

"I can't be with you and give my family a hundred percent at the same time. My feelings for you run way too deep. I have to let you go, Caesar. Besides, you deserve so much more than only a part of me."

"I can't let you go. I fell in love the moment I laid eyes on you. To get you and then to lose you. I can't let that happen."

"If you truly love me like you say you do, then you will. Think about Ashton and how much she needs her mother and her father to be united as one. My daughter is sick. If we don't get her the help she needs, her life is over."

"Fuuuuuuck!" Caesar balled up his fists and stood up. "You really doing this to me to us. I wanna hate you so bad right now but I don't, I love you even more. Some muthafuckers have all the luck and Allen Collins would be one of them."

"Would it be completely selfish of me, to ask that we make love one last time?" Karmen didn't want to give Caesar up either but she was willing to sacrifice him, to save her daughter.

"I would give anything to be inside you right now but I'm afraid I won't let you go. I'll be on some hold you hostage type shit," he chuckled. "But I'm dead ass," Caesar stated.

But Caesar couldn't resist stepping closer to his lady love and he leaned down placing his face near her neck. The seductive scent of her perfume would get him every time. Then he brushed the tip of his nose against her hair and it had this fresh, clean smell. He was battling with his emotions and the shit had him trippin'. Karmen was no longer listening to reason but at this point, he was all caught up. There was no sense in talking. Caesar decided to put it down, make it the best though and accept this would be the last time.

Ashton got out the car and walked towards the front door of the Tanglewood Spanish inspired home that was tucked away on an expansive corner. Upon entry, there was a library with a fireplace to the right and a lavish dining room with a handcrafted Italian chandelier, faux finished ceiling and marble flooring, overlooking a private courtyard and tree lined yard. Their elaborate new home was breathtaking. The last time she was there, she didn't have a chance to appreciate it. Her and Damacio got into a heated argument over her drug use and she ran out in tears but Ashton knew this time would be different. She wanted her husband back and was here to tell Damacio, she was ready to do what was necessary for that to happen.

"Ashton, what are you doing here?" she turned in the direction of Damacio's voice.

"Good morning," Ashton smiled. "I wanted to come see my husband." As she walked towards Damacio, she froze. It felt like a sharp knife had been lunged into her heart.

"Damacio, do you have a shirt I can put on?" the naked woman asked as she came down the stairwell.

"Oh, I didn't realize you had company."

"Go back upstairs. I'll be there in a minute," Damacio told the leggy beauty, who quickly disappeared.

"It's crazy because a few weeks ago, I told Vannette not to show up to my brother's house unannounced because there was no telling what she might see. I guess I should've taken my own advice. But this is my house too and you are my husband, so I didn't think those same rules applied to me. You proved me wrong," Ashton's voice cracked.

"I told you I was done with you. Maybe now you believe me," Damacio said, coldly.

"How can you stand there and break my heart like this. You brought another woman into our house, in our bed. You could've at least changed the locks, so I wouldn't have walked in on you and her."

"But yet, you had no problem being out in public with another man. Kissing him, letting him have his hands all over you, doing coke. I know how you get when you're high. I'm sure you fucked him too."

"Damacio, I was wrong for all of that but I swear, I never had sex with him. I haven't been with another man since you. I haven't wanted to. You were everything I needed and ever wanted."

"Not everything. That white powder had way more influence over you than I ever did."

"If this had been a week ago, I would've flipped out coming here finding you with another woman. I would've tried to destroy everything in this house, including you and her. And afterwards, I'd do a ton of coke while partying all night, without a care in the world but not anymore."

"Is this the part where you say, I won. Now, I'm free to be with all the women I want and you're free to do all the coke you like...huh, Ashton!"

"Yes and no. Damacio, you are free to be with whatever woman you want but I'm done with the coke and the drugs. I came here to tell you I'm going to rehab. My mother found a great treatment center for me in Ventura, California. My flight leaves tonight. I wanted to save our marriage but more importantly, I need to save my life."

"Ashton, wait." Damacio reached out for her arm, as she walked past him to leave.

"What is it?"

Damacio was compelled to tell his wife, how much he still loved her and they would work at saving their marriage once she got back from rehab. But instead of pouring out his heart, he held back.

"I hope you get the help you need during your stay at rehab." Damacio stated, letting Ashton walk out the door.

Chapter Nineteen

Redemption

"How hard can it be for you to find a Spanish nigga that go by Chi? I'm not understanding this shit!" Caesar spit over the phone. "Them yo' fuckin' people."

"I'm workin' on it but so far I get nothing," Pedro, the dude Caesar hired to locate Chi, grumbled.

"I tell you what. Try this. Start asking around about a kidnapping, of a young black female, from a very wealthy and prominent family in Houston. See if anyone heard who got paid to do the job."

"Oh, you never told me this. That's helpful info!"

Pedro exclaimed. "If this Chi person was the kidnapper, he probably not say his real name."

"Yeah...yeah...yeah," Caesar agreed. "That's why I want you to switch shit up. I thought maybe you could find him off a nickname, since you be in the streets wit' a lot of them cats but since that ain't workin', try this."

"This is good. I'm on it, Caesar. I won't let you down. I wanna do real business wit' you. I'm valuable," Pedro insisted.

"Don't talk about it...prove it. Next time I hear from you, have some real info for me," Caesar said, putting the pressure on Pedro before hanging up.

"You sure you wanna do this?" Darius questioned. "I mean this Chi nigga work for Alejo, who is our supplier. You kill his men, that shit ain't gon' sit well wit' him."

"I'll handle Alejo but them niggas gon' die. I won't let the nigga Chi be tortured because he did keep Ashton from being raped. But the other muthafucka gon' suffer. Ain't no changing my mind on that shit."

"You do know, this still ain't gonna make that lady leave her husband and come back to you."

"You don't know that shit for sure," Caesar shot back.

"Man, them types ain't like us. They come from a different world. I get her husband sell drugs like we do but he's crossed to the other side. He's a well-known and respected businessman and his wife has been groomed to play her role. She's not leaving him, for you or for anybody." Darius tried to make his friend understand.

"Maybe you right but I gotta at least try. I was this close," Caesar put a small space between his thumb and index finger, "To making Karmen mine. We fell in love."

"Nigga, do you hear yo'self? You ain't neva been in love wit' nothin' but the fuckin' game, yo' whole damn life. You sound crazy right now!" Darius shook his head, not understanding the words coming out of his friend's mouth.

"Nah, I never thought it would happen either but it's real, we're in love."

"No, you infatuated. There's a difference," Darius cautioned. "You been obsessed wit' that lady since she walked into the hotel. I get it. She's that unobtainable type woman, you never thought you could get but let it go. At least you fulfilled part of the fantasy. Ya done had sex and all that good shit. Most muthafuckas never get that far. Be happy and move the fuck on, before you take this shit too far!" Darius warned.

"I hear you but let me do me. I ain't made it this far in life, by not knowing when shit has been taken too far. I got this!"

From the grimace expression on Caesar's face, Darius knew not to push his friend any further. Once he set his mind on something, he was determined to see it through. Darius would have to let Caesar do exactly that, even if the ending result proved to be fatal.

"You look just as beautiful, if not more than on the day we first met all those years ago," Allen complimented, kissing his wife's hand.

"Thank you," Karmen said, glancing in the mirror one last time, before they left out for the dinner party they were attending.

"When I picked out this dress, I knew it would look perfect on you." Allen placed his hands on his wife's shoulders, this time kissing her neck, admiring the mauve, floral embroidered gown with a mermaid silhouette she was wearing. There was a mesh cutout with thin spaghetti straps which emphasized her delicate collarbone.

"You've always had impeccable taste," Karmen managed to say, although her body almost froze at her husband's touch. She'd become accustomed to Caesar's hands making love to every inch of her body. Having Allen this close, had become almost foreign to her but she was willing to try.

"Stay right there," Allen said, disappearing into his custom walk-in closet. He returned soon after holding a long black jewelry box. He took out the diamond round, pear marquise center drop necklace and placed it around his wife's neck.

"Oh my Allen, this is gorgeous." Karmen had an endless amount of jewelry but was stunned by the 56 carat platinum choker. "What's the occasion?"

"Have I ever needed an occasion to get my beautiful wife jewelry?" Allen kissed Karmen on the lips. Each kiss, he hoped was getting him closer to making love to his wife once again.

"No you haven't."

"It might not be an occasion but I do have a reason."

"Which is?" she questioned.

"I want to thank you for not giving up on me and our marriage. I know I've put you through a lot this past year but you're the only woman who has ever had my heart and I know I'm the only man who has ever had yours. We belong together and I'm grateful you finally accepted that."

"Yes, I have accepted we belong together. We should go. We don't want to be late for the dinner party," Karmen said, taking her husband's hand.

Karmen kept reminding herself, she was the wife of Allen Collins and the mother of his children. Her loyalty was to her family and nothing or no one could supersede that, not even her love for Caesar. It took all her strength to stay away and not call him but it's what she had to do, to keep her family close.

"Girl, so sorry I'm running late but it took me forever to find something to wear tonight," Crystal said to Remi, as she was walking to her car.

"Well, you better hurry up! You know the traffic

is gonna be ridiculous. I don't want to miss the show not even the opening act!" Remi shouted through the phone.

"Calm yo' ass down! I'm coming. My hair and makeup is done. All I have to do is change my clothes and we out. See you in a minute," Crystal said, ending the call and tossing it in her purse. She was so engrossed in her conversation with Remi, Crystal hadn't noticed a sedan circling around the block, watching her every step.

"Fuck! I bet that's Remi calling me back," Crystal smacked, fidgeting in her purse to retrieve her phone but instead of getting it, everything fell on the pavement. "Dammit! This isn't my fuckin' day," she fussed, bending down to pick up her belongings.

It wasn't until the bright headlights blinded her, did Crystal even have an inclination she'd been targeted. She put up her hands to block the glare and try to see but the lights were too bright. Then she heard a car door open and a familiar face stepped out the light.

"Jackson, what are you doing here?" Crystal was confused.

"Mr. Collins wants to make sure you don't cause any more problems for his family."

"I'm not. I haven't been in contact with anyone, including Kasir."

"He wants to guarantee it stays that way." Crystal wasn't given an opportunity to plead her case. She'd been tried and convicted in the eyes of Allen Collins and that's all Jackson needed to know. He pumped three bullets in Crystal's chest. Leaving her bloody body, slumped on the parking lot pavement.

"Mr. Collins, it's done." Jackson called his boss and told him, as he drove off into the night.

Chapter Twenty

The Battle Begins

"Dinner was delicious, Vannette. I'm so used to eating out, I forgot how nice it was to sit down at the dinner table. I used to do it all the time, when I lived at home with my parents," Clayton said, putting down his napkin.

"Do you miss that?"

"Sometimes but only because of my mother."

"You two really are close."

"Yes. She's an incredible woman and mother."

"Hopefully I will be too." Vannette's comment was so subtle, Clayton almost missed it.

"I'm sure whenever you decide to have kids, you'll be a great mother too."

"I guess we'll be finding out soon because I'm pregnant," Vannette announced.

"Excuse me?"

"It must've happened that day you came to my apartment. It was the only time we didn't use protection."

"I remember that day vividly," Clayton stood up and said. "Are you sure?"

"Positive. Clayton, I know you wasn't expecting this but I really want to have this baby and I want you to be a part of our lives."

"Vannette, I need a moment." Clayton walked over to the couch in the living room and sat down. He put his head down and let out a deep sigh. He wasn't ready for this but what Clayton was about to say next would change everything.

"Clayton, I know you're probably overwhelmed right now but..."

"This can be dealt with," he said, interrupting Vannette. "I was raised in a home with both my parents and so will my child."

"You want us to live together?" A smiled crept across Vannette's face.

"No, I want us to get married."

"You're asking me to be your wife?!" Vannette gasped, damn near falling out her chair.

"Yes, it's the right thing to do for our child."

"I'm stunned right now. I've been wanting to tell you since I found out a week ago but I was so nervous. I thought you'd be furious. Never in my wildest dream, did I think you'd ask me to be your wife." Vannette's face lit up with excitement.

"Vannette, you know me and my lifestyle. It's the reason I think this arrangement can work. I care about you and I'll make sure you're provided for as my wife but don't expect for me to change," Clayton clarified. "If you can't handle that, tell me now."

"It's not the ideal situation but you know how much I love you. I would be honored to be your wife but I do have one request."

"What is it?"

"I can deal with the other women but not Brianna. Please stop seeing her. She used to be my friend. I can't handle having my husband and the father of my child, continue seeing someone I feel betrayed me. Please Clayton," Vannette pleaded.

Clayton bit down on his lip and stared up at the ceiling fan. It was obvious he was struggling with the request.

"You care about her don't you?" Vannette asked, although she knew the answer.

"Yeah, I do but you're carrying my child and what you need comes first."

"Does that mean you'll leave her alone?"

"Yes, Vannette I'll leave Brianna alone." Clayton got up from the couch and walked over to her. "I don't want you stressing about unimportant shit like that," he said, kissing her forehead. "You're having my baby. You have to focus on staying healthy for our unborn child."

"You promise, Clayton?"

"Yes, I promise. I'll end my relationship with Brianna."

"Thank you. I'm going to be a wonderful mother and an excellent wife. You'll see." Vannette's desire to please Clayton was evident.

"I know you will."

"You said this is more like an arrangement but will we at least have a wedding?" Vannette questioned.

"Baby, of course. You can have the biggest wedding you want. You'll be my wife and entitled to every perk that comes with that."

"Thank you so much, Clayton." Vannette reached up and kissed her future husband. In awe that all her dreams were coming true.

"Anything for the mother of my child," he smiled until the doorbell ringing got his attention. "Who could that be," Clayton wondered, going to answer the door.

"Hi. I know I shouldn't have just popped up but this couldn't wait."

"Brianna, this really isn't a good time," Clayton said, trying to keep Vannette from hearing her voice.

"Clayton, who's at the door?" Vannette was curious to know, coming closer. "What is Brianna doing here?"

"She was just leaving," Clayton told Vannette. He

didn't want any drama between the ladies.

"No, let her come in. I want to share our news." Vannette gave a wicked smile.

"I don't think this is the right time." Clayton stated.

"You made a promise to me. Now is as good a time as any to keep it." Vannette wasn't going to let an opportunity to stick it to her nemesis pass her by.

"Come on in," Clayton said, reluctantly.

"What news did you want to share with me, Vannette?" Brianna asked once inside.

"Before Vannette shares her news, can you tell me what was so important, you had to come over here tonight?" Clayton did want to know, plus he was also looking for an excuse to prolong breaking the news to Brianna, their relationship was over.

"If you don't mind, can I talk to you in private?" Brianna preferred.

"Whatever you have to tell Clayton, you can say in front of me." Vannette stood beside him, staking her claim.

"Fine, if you insist." Brianna wasn't going to argue. "Clayton, you're going to be a father. We're having a baby."

"You liar!" Vannette lunged at Brianna. Clayton put up his arm, blocking Vannette from making contact.

"I'm not lying. I even bought another pregnancy test before I came over here, in case Clayton didn't believe me," Brainna told them.

"Of course you knew he wouldn't believe you because it isnt' true!" Vannette shouted.

"If you're so sure, Vannette, you can come in the bathroom with me and watch me piss on the stick," Brianna offered smugly.

"How did this happen. Besides that one time, which was months ago, I always used protection," Clayton sighed. News of one baby was enough to deal with, now there were two.

"Condoms aren't full proof and I'm not on the pill. I guess it was meant to be," Brianna said sweetly. "Now what news did you want to share with me, Vannette? I'm sure it won't trump mine."

"Vannette, is pregnant too," Clayton revealed, feeling like he was in the twilight zone.

"Yes, I am!" Vannette snapped at Brianna. "Clayton also asked me to be his wife because he wanted our child to be raised in a home with both their parents."

"If that's the case, then I guess Clayton has to marry me too. Don't you want the same thing for our baby?" Brianna locked eyes with Clayton forcing him to respond.

"Your pregnancy doesn't change anything, Brianna!" Vannette screamed.

"Vannette, that's enough." Clayton put his hand up. "Brianna's pregnancy does change things. I can't put one child before the other."

"So what are you going to do?" Brianna and Vannette asked in unison.

The women waited anxiously for his response. They both wanted the number one position in Clayton's life, even if they had to share him. Unbeknownst to Vannette, her accidental pregnancy gave her a shot at claiming that spot. Brianna on the other hand, created her chance through good old fashion scheming.

It didn't take Brianna long to figure out, Clayton was a player and had no intentions of slowing down. She didn't want to risk him eventually losing interest and replacing her with someone else, so she began plotting a way to make herself a permanent fixture in his life. Brianna didn't want to gamble on it happening the conventional way, since Clayton was an avid condom user. She had to get crafty and resorted to trap a nigga rule #101: after having sex, confiscate the used condom. It took Brianna multiple tries but she finally struck gold. Just in time too, since she was on the verge of being dismissed. Now she was back in the race and ready to knock Vannette down to the number two slot.

When Caesar pulled up to the sprawling estate that rested on top of a bluff, thoroughly impressed didn't do his feelings justice. Although he was in love with the man's wife, Caesar also greatly admired and respected everything Allen Collins had accomplished. He represented the epitome of reaching the ultimate level of success and Caesar had no qualms about giving credit where credit was due. He also had no qualms about turning the business mogul's world upside down.

"Yes, may I help you?" Ms. Bernice opened the door, greeting Caesar.

"Good evening. My name is Caesar and I'm here to see Allen Collins."

"Is Mr. Collins expecting you?"

"No but tell him, I'm here regarding his daughter Ashton."

"Of course." Ms. Bernice politely invited the handsome man in and went to let Mr. Collins know he had a visitor.

While he waited, Caesar stood in the foyer, taking in the stunning floating grand staircases, the lavish gilt and delicately wrought, hand painted detail, meticulously reproduced period moldings, white marble tile and inlaid, hand scraped hardwood floors, antique boiserie, chandeliers and marble fireplaces. Their home was a showcase of pure opulence.

"Hello Caesar." Allen Collins walked in the foyer and stood. "I'm told your visit is in regards to my daughter Ashton."

"Yes, it is." Caesar nodded. He walked closer and as he expected the man he heard so much about, had a commanding presence.

"Might I ask, how you know my daughter?"

"We have mutual acquaintances."

"I see. Well, I'm listening. What information do you

have about Ashton?"

"I know it wasn't Alejo Hernandez who had your daughter kidnapped. It was you." Caesar stated brazenly. "Would you like to be the one to tell your wife you orchestrated Ashton's abduction, or should I?"

Caesar stood firm in his question, as he and the man he despised but also admired, were standing eye to eye. A war had been unleashed and Caesar knew Allen Collins would prove to be his toughest adversary. Their feud was destined to be nothing short of epic.

Coming Soon... The Final Installment

A KING PRODUCTION

Baller

Bitches

THE REUNION

VOLUME 4

JOY DEJA KING

Chapter One

Nothing Seems To Be The Same

The gray skies filled with heavy clouds on the cold winter day satirized the grief looming in the air. The low rumble of distant thunder could be heard as guests arrived for the outdoor graveside funeral service.

"Do you think Blair and Kennedy are coming?" Diamond asked Cameron as they took their seats.

"Honestly..."

"Look," Diamond cut her husband off as she nodded her head towards the arriving cars. "It's

Kennedy. She came," Diamond said smiling. *Please God, let Blair show up too,* she prayed to herself.

As if the angels heard her pleas, a few minutes later a chauffeur-driven, black tinted Rolls Royce Phantom pulled up.

"Mommy, mommy, Auntie Blair is here!" Elijah exclaimed when she stepped out the car. "Do you think Donovan came?"

"I don't think so, sweetie." Diamond smiled, patting her son's head.

"I still can't believe she went back to that dude," Cameron shook his head and said as Blair and Skee Patron arrived hand in hand.

"All that matters is that she showed up... both of them," Diamond said, thrilled to see her best friends.

It had been a year since Diamond had spoken to Blair or Kennedy. Never did she imagine their reunion would take place at a funeral. Life had torn them apart, it seemed it took death to bring them back together.

A KING PRODUCTION
Rich or Famous
Rich Because You Can Buy Fame
A NOVEL
JOY DEJA KING

Lorenzo

Welcome To My World

★★★★

Before I die, if you don't remember anything else I ever taught you, know this. A man will be judged, not on what he has but how much of it. So you find a way to make money and when you think you've made enough, make some more, because you'll need it to survive in this cruel world. Money will be the only thing to save you. As I sat across from Darnell those words my father said to me on his deathbed played in my head.

"Yo, Lorenzo, are you listening to me, did you hear anything I said?"

"I heard everything you said. The problem for you is I don't give a fuck." I responded, giving a casual shoulder shrug as I rested my thumb under my chin with my index finger above my mouth.

"What you mean, you don't give a fuck? We been doing business for over three years now and that's the best you got for me?"

"Here's the thing, Darnell, I got informants all over these streets. As a matter of fact that broad you've had in your back pocket for the last few weeks is one of them."

"I don't understand what you saying," Darnell said swallowing hard. He tried to keep the tone of his voice calm, but his body composure was speaking something different.

"Alexus, has earned every dollar I've paid her to fuck wit' yo' blood suckin' ass. You a fake fuck wit' no fangs. You wanna play wit' my 100 g's like you at the casino. That's a real dummy move, Darnell." I could see the sweat beads gathering, resting in the creases of Darnell's forehead.

"Lorenzo, man, I don't know what that bitch told you but none of it is true! I swear 'bout four niggas ran up in my crib last night and took all my shit. Now that I think about it, that trifling ho Alexus probably had me set up! She fucked us both over!"

I shook my head for a few seconds not believing this muthafucker was saying that shit with a straight face. "I thought you said it was two niggas that ran up in your crib now that shit done doubled. Next thing you gon' spit is that all of Marcy projects was in on the stickup."

"Man, I can get your money. I can have it to you first thing tomorrow. I swear!"

"The thing is I need my money right now." I casually stood up from my seat and walked towards Darnell who now looked like he had been dipped in water. Watching him fall apart in front of my eyes made up for the fact that I would never get back a dime of the money he owed me.

"Zo, you so paid, this shit ain't gon' even faze you. All I'm asking for is less than twenty-four hours. You can at least give me that," Darnell pleaded.

"See, that's your first mistake, counting my pockets. My money is *my* money, so yes this shit do faze me."

"I didn't mean it like that. I wasn't tryna disrespect you. By this time tomorrow you will have your money and we can put this shit behind us." Darnell's eyes darted around in every direction instead of looking directly at me. A good liar, he was not.

"Since you were robbed of the money you owe me and the rest of my drugs, how you gon' get me my dough? I mean the way you tell it, they didn't leave you wit' nothin' but yo' dirty draws."

"I'll work it out. Don't even stress yourself, I got you, man."

"What you saying is that the nigga you so called aligned yourself with, by using my money and my product, is going to hand it back over to you?"

"Zo, what you talking 'bout? I ain't aligned myself wit' nobody. That slaw ass bitch Alexus feeding you lies."

"No, that's you feeding me lies. Why don't you admit you no longer wanted to work for me? You felt you was big shit and could be your own boss. So you used my money and product to buy your way in with this other nigga to step in my territory. But you ain't no boss you a poser. And your need to perpetrate a fraud is going to cost you your life."

"Lorenzo, don't do this man! This is all a big misunderstanding. I swear on my daughter I will have your money tomorrow. Fuck, if you let me leave right now I'll have that shit to you tonight!" I listened to Darnell stutter his words.

My men, who had been patiently waiting in each corner of the warehouse, dressed in all black, loaded with nothing but artillery, stepped out of the darkness ready to obliterate the enemy I had once considered my best worker. Darnell's eyes widened as he witnessed the men who had saved and protected him on numerous occasions, as he dealt with the vultures he encountered in the street life, now ready to end his.

"Don't do this, Zo! Pleeease," Darnell was now on his knees begging.

"Damn, nigga, you already a thief and a backstabber. Don't add, going out crying like a bitch to that too. Man the fuck up. At least take this bullet like a soldier."

"I'm sorry, Zo. Please don't do this. I gotta daughter that need me. Pleeease man, I'll do anything. Just don't kill me." The tears were pouring down Darnell's face and instead of softening me up it just made me even more pissed at his punk ass.

"Save your fuckin' tears. You shoulda thought about your daughter before you stole from me. You're the worse sort of thief. I invite you into my home, I make you a part of my family and you steal from me, you plot against me. Your daughter doesn't need you. You have nothing to teach her."

My men each pulled out their gat ready to attack and I put my hand up motioning them to stop. For the first time since Darnell arrived, a calm gaze spread across his face.

"I knew you didn't have the heart to let them kill me, Zo. We've been through so much together. I mean you Tania's God Father. We bigger than this and we will get through it," Darnell said, halfway smiling as he began getting off his knees and standing up.

"You're right, I don't have the heart to let them kill you, I'ma do that shit myself." Darnell didn't even have a chance to let what I said resonate with him because I just sprayed that muthafucker like the piece of shit he was. "Clean this shit up," I said, stepping over Darnell's bullet ridden body as I made my exit.

A KING PRODUCTION

MEN OF
The Bitch Series
AND THE WOMEN WHO
Love Them

JOY DEJA KING

Chapter One

Adrenaline Rush

Before Precious Cummings stole their hearts, there was another woman both Nico Carter and Supreme shared. But until this day, they never knew it. Her name was Vandresse Lawson and although she loved them both, she was only in love with herself and it cost her everything.

"Girl, that color is poppin'. I think I need to

get that too," Tanica said, eyeing her friend's nail polish as the Chinese lady was polishing them.

"You bet not! We ain't gon' be walking around here wit' the same color polish on," Vandresse huffed.

"Won't nobody be paying attention to that shit," Tanica said, sucking her teeth.

"Stop it!" Vandresse frowned up her face as if. "You know everybody around here pay attention to what I do. All these chicks dying to be just like me," she boasted, admiring how the plum polish made her honey-colored skin pop.

Tanica glanced over at her best friend and rolled her eyes. She loved Vandresse like a sister, but at the same time Tanica felt she was so full of shit. But there was no denying, in the streets of Harlem: Vandresse was the queen of this shit. She was always the real pretty girl in the neighborhood, but once she started fuckin' with that nigga Courtney, it was on. Nobody could tell her nothing, including her childhood friend Tanica.

"I'll take that pink color," Tanica told the lady doing her nails. She had no desire to beef with Vandresse over something as simple as polish.

"So are we going to the club tonight or what?" she asked ready to talk about having some fun.

"I can't." Vandresse sighed.

"Why not? We've been talking about hitting this club since we first heard they was reopening it weeks ago."

"I know, but I told Courtney we would hang out tonight."

"Ya always hang out. Can't you spend a little time with your best friend?"

"Maybe tomorrow. I mean look at this tennis bracelet he got me." Vandresse held up her arm and slowly twirled her wrist like she was waving in a beauty pageant. "These diamonds are stunning. If I have to spend some quality time wit' my man, give him some head, sex him real good so the gifts keep coming, you gotta understand that," Vandresse explained with no filter as if the nail salon wasn't full of people, but of course she didn't give a fuck.

"I get it. I just miss hanging out with you. Brittany is cool, but she's not as fun as you," Tanica hated to admit.

"Of course she isn't, but it's not her fault. I'm the turn up queen." Vandresse laughed.

"Yeah you are." Tanica joined in on the laugh.

"But on the real. I miss hanging out with you too even though we're roommates and attend hair school together. But we haven't just hung out and had some fun like we used to. I wish Courtney had a cute friend I could hook you up with."

"Me too. Because that one you hooked me up with last time was not the answer."

"I know, but I was hoping his money would help you excuse his face," Vandresse said shrugging.

"How you luck out and get a dude who's cute and got money," Tanica stated shaking her head. "I can't believe out of all the friends Courtney got ain't none of them good looking."

"That's not true. One of his friends is a real cutie, but he just a low level worker. But he can afford to take you out to eat and buy you some sneakers... stuff like that. At least we would be able to do some double dating. If you want me to hook you up just say the word."

"Let me think about it. I don't know if I wanna sit around watching yo' man shower you wit' diamonds, all while homeboy taking me to

Footlocker, so I can pick out a new pair of Nikes."

"You so crazy." Vandresse giggled before both girls burst out laughing while continuing to chat and make jokes while finishing up at the nail salon.

"I figured you would wanna chill tonight," Vandresse said looking in the passenger side mirror as she put on some more lip gloss. "I did say I was gonna treat you extra special tonight for icing out my wrist so lovely." She smiled, using the tip of her freshly manicured nail to tap the diamonds on her tennis bracelet.

"I didn't forget. I'ma hold you to that." Courtney winked, squeezing Vandresse's bare upper thigh. "But umm, I told my man Anton I would stop by for a second. He poppin' some bottles for his birthday. Nothing major. He keepin' low key. But we do a lot of business together and I promised I come through."

"I feel you." Vandresse smiled not really caring either way. She was already plotting on how she was going to suck his dick so good tonight so she could get a diamond ring to go with her bracelet.

"But when we leave here, it's back to the crib so you can take care of Daddy." Courtney nodded.

"You know I got you, baby." Vandresse licked her lips thinking how lucky she was to have a sexy nigga who could fuck and was getting money out in these streets.

When they walked into the Uptown lounge it was jammed pack. "I thought you said this was low key," Vandresse commented.

"A lot of niggas fuck wit' Anton so they all probably coming through to show love," Courtney replied as he headed straight to the back like he knew exactly where he was going. Vandresse was right by his side, happy that she decided to wear a sexy dress tonight since there was a gang of chicks in the spot. When it came to stuntin' on other bitches, Vandresse was super competitive. She always wanted to be number one or at the very least top three.

"My nigga, C!" A guy who Vandresse assumed was the birthday boy stood up showing Courtney love.

"Happy birthday, man!" Courtney grinned. "I see everybody came out to show love to my homie."

"Yeah, I wasn't expecting all these people, but hey it's my birthday! You and your lady sit down and have some champagne," Anton said, playing the perfect host.

Courtney took Vandresse's hand so they could sit down. "Baby, I'll be right back. I need to go to the restroom. Have a glass of bubbly waiting for me when I get back," she said kissing him on the cheek.

"Excuse me, where's the restroom?" Vandresse asked one of the cocktail waitresses. The lady pointed up the stairs so Vandresse headed in that direction.

When she got to the bathroom, Vandresse was relieved nobody was in there. She wanted to check to make sure one of her tracks hadn't came loose. Vandresse always kept a needle and some thread in her purse just in case. She examined her weave and to her relief it wasn't a loose track brushing against her ear, it was her leave out. Vandresse glanced at her reflection one last time and after feeling confident she had her shit together, she exited out right as a handful of chicks were coming in.

Right in the entry way of the bathroom there was a huge spotlight. When Vandresse came in, the upstairs was damn near empty, but when she came out, there were a ton of people and all eyes seemed to be fixated on her. *Thank goodness I made sure I was straight before I walked out*, Vandresse thought to herself. She was heading back down stairs when she felt a firm grasp on her arm.

"Why the fu..." before Vandresse had a chance to curse the man out, she locked eyes with a nigga so fine she changed her mind.

"I apologize for grabbing on you, but I couldn't let you get away. You are beautiful. What's your name?"

"Vandresse," she uttered. The man's intense stare had her feeling self-conscious for some reason. Like his eyes were piercing through her soul.

"My name is Nico. Nico Carter. Come sit

down with me so we can have a drink." He spoke with so much confidence that Vandresse found herself following behind the stranger like her man wasn't downstairs waiting for her.

"I'm sorry. I can't go with you," she finally said, snapping out of her trance.

"No need to apologize. Did I do or say something to offend you?" Nico questioned.

"Not at all. I'm actually here with my man. He's downstairs waiting for me."

"Oh, really," Nico said unmoved. "That might be a problem for you tonight, but it doesn't have to be tomorrow."

Vandresse gave Nico a quizzical look. "I'm not following you."

"You're not wearing a wedding ring so you not married. Are you willing to miss out on what might be the best thing that ever happened to you?"

"Wow, you're a little full of yourself."

"Only because I have every reason to be. Give me your phone number. I'm more of an action person than a talker."

Vandresse wanted to say no because she had a good thing going with Courtney, but she also knew it wasn't a sure thing. Like Nico said, he wasn't her husband and they were both young. Vandresse wasn't stupid. She was well aware Courtney was still out there doing him. Vandresse knew she was his main bitch, but not his only chick.

"Here," she said, writing her number on a napkin then handing it to Nico.

"You're smart and beautiful. I think we'll get along just fine."

"We shall see. But I gotta go."

"Cool, I'll call you tomorrow." Nico stood at the top of the stairs looking over the banister and watched Vandresse walk over to a small group of people. A young dude stood up and took her hand and he figured that must be her man. Nico knew he needed to leave that alone, but the same way he got an adrenaline rush from dealing drugs, chasing a beautiful woman that was technically unavailable gave Nico that same high.

A KING PRODUCTION

Bad Bitches Only

ASSASSINS...

EPISODE 1
(Be Careful With Me)

JOY DEJA KING

Chapter One

HE LOVES ME

Bailey strutted out the Hartsfield-Jackson Atlanta International Airport, in her strappy, four inch snakeskin shoes, wearing matte black wire frame square sunglas ses and a designer suit tailored to fit her size six frame perfectly. The brown beauty looked like she was a partner at a powerful law firm, when actually she was barely a second year law student. But school was the least of her worries. Bailey had other things on her mind, like the promise ring she was wearing. It cost more than some people's home. Don't get it confused, this wasn't a promise of sexual abstinence. This was a promise of marriage, from her boyfriend of five years, Dino Jacobs.

"Keera," I was just about to call you girl," Bailey said, getting in her car.

"I was shocked as shit when you answered. I was expecting to leave a voicemail. You said you was gonna be in some conferences all day," Keera replied.

"Girl, I was but I checked out early. I'm back in the A."

"You back in Atlanta?!" Keera questioned, sounding surprised.

"Yep. That's why I was calling you. So we could do drinks later on tonight at that spot we like." Baily was getting hyped, as she was dropping the top on her Lunar Blue Metallic E 400 Benz.

"Most definitely...so where you headed now."

"Where you think...home to my man! Stop playin'," Bailey laughed, getting on interstate 75.

"I know yo' boo, will be happy to see you."

"Yep and his ass gon' be surprised too. He thinks I'm coming back tomorrow night. But I missed my baby. Plus that conference was boring as hell. All them snobby ass lawyers was workin' my nerves."

"Get used to it, cause you about to be one," Keera reminded her.

"Yeah but only cause Dino insisted. You know

I wanted to attend beauty school. I love all things hair and makeup. I have zero interest in law. But that nigga the one paying for it, so it's whatever," Bailey smacked.

"Girl, don't be wasting that man money. You better get yo' law degree and handle them cases!" Keera giggled.

"Okaaaay!! I believe Dino just want me to be able to represent his ass, in case anything go down," Bailey snickered.

"Well, let me get off the phone so you can get home."

"Keera, I know how to talk and drive at the same damn time," she popped.

"I didn't say you didn't but umm I have a nail appointment. You know they be swamped on a Friday," Keera explained.

"True. Okay, go get yo' raggedy nails done," Bailey joked. "Call me later, so we can decide what time we meeting for drinks."

"Will do! Talk to you later on."

When Bailey got off the phone with Keera, she immediately started blasting some Cardi B. The music, mixed with the nice summer breeze blowing through her hair, had her feeling sexy. She began imagining the dick down she'd get from Dino, soon as she got home.

"Here I come baby," Bailey smiled, pulling in the driveway. She was practically skipping inside the house and up the stairs, giddy like a silly schoolgirl. You'd think hearing Silk's old school Freak Me, echoing down the hallway, in the middle of the afternoon, would've sent the alarm ringing in Bailey's head. Instead, it made her try to reach her man faster.

It wasn't until she got a few steps from the slightly ajar bedroom door, did her heart start racing. Next came the rapid breathing and finally came dread. You know the type of dread, that seems like it's worse than death but you don't know for sure because you've never actually died. It was all too much for Bailey. Her eyes were bleeding blood. She wanted to erase everything she just witnessed and rewind time.

I shoulda kept my ass in DC, she screamed to herself, heading back downstairs and leaving the house. Once outside, Bailey started to vomit in the bushes, until there was nothing left in her stomach.

P.O. Box 912
Collierville, TN 38027

A KING PRODUCTION

www.joydejaking.com
www.twitter.com/joydejaking

ORDER FORM

Name:

Address:

City/State:

Zip:

QUANTITY	TITLES	PRICE	TOTAL
	Bitch	$15.00	
	Bitch Reloaded	$15.00	
	The Bitch Is Back	$15.00	
	Queen Bitch	$15.00	
	Last Bitch Standing	$15.00	
	Superstar	$15.00	
	Ride Wit' Me	$12.00	
	Ride Wit' Me Part 2	$15.00	
	Stackin' Paper	$15.00	
	Trife Life To Lavish	$15.00	
	Trife Life To Lavish II	$15.00	
	Stackin' Paper II	$15.00	
	Rich or Famous	$15.00	
	Rich or Famous Part 2	$15.00	
	Rich or Famous Part 3	$15.00	
	Bitch A New Beginning	$15.00	
	Mafia Princess Part 1	$15.00	
	Mafia Princess Part 2	$15.00	
	Mafia Princess Part 3	$15.00	
	Mafia Princess Part 4	$15.00	
	Mafia Princess Part 5	$15.00	
	Boss Bitch	$15.00	
	Baller Bitches Vol. 1	$15.00	
	Baller Bitches Vol. 2	$15.00	
	Baller Bitches Vol. 3	$15.00	
	Bad Bitch	$15.00	
	Still The Baddest Bitch	$15.00	
	Power	$15.00	
	Power Part 2	$15.00	
	Drake	$15.00	
	Drake Part 2	$15.00	
	Female Hustler	$15.00	
	Female Hustler Part 2	$15.00	
	Female Hustler Part 3	$15.00	
	Female Hustler Part 4	$15.00	
	Female Hustler Part 5	$15.00	
	Female Hustler Part 6	$15.00	
	Princess Fever "Birthday Bash"	$9.99	
	Nico Carter The Men Of The Bitch Series	$15.00	
	Bitch The Beginning Of The End	$15.00	
	Supreme...Men Of The Bitch Series	$15.00	
	Bitch The Final Chapter	$15.00	
	Stackin' Paper III	$15.00	
	Men Of The Bitch Series And The Women Who Love Them	$15.00	
	Coke Like The 80s	$15.00	
	Baller Bitches The Reunion Vol. 4	$15.00	
	Stackin' Paper IV	$15.00	
	The Legacy	$15.00	
	Lovin' Thy Enemy	$15.00	
	Stackin' Paper V	$15.00	
	The Legacy Part 2	$15.00	

Shipping/Handling (Via Priority Mail) $7.50 1-2 Books, $15.00 3-4 Books add $1.95 for ea. Additional book.
Total: $_____ FORMS OF ACCEPTED PAYMENTS: Certified or government issued checks and money Orders, all mail in orders take 5-7 Business days to be delivered

CPSIA information can be obtained
at www.ICGtesting.com
Printed in the USA
LVHW051658300120
645335LV00003B/367